the Same
Rainbow's End

Also by Mary Cates

The Wonted Voice of Forgiveness

Hidden in Irish Hills

the Same Rainbow's End

A NOVEL

MARY CATES

Ambassador International
GREENVILLE, SOUTH CAROLINA & BELFAST, NORTHERN IRELAND

www.ambassador-international.com

The Same Rainbow's End

ISBN: 978-1-64960-351-7
eISBN: 978-1-64960-368-5
Library of Congress Control Number: 2022938910

Editing by Katie Cruice Smith
Cover design by Hannah Linder Designs
Interior typesetting by Dentelle Design

Scripture taken from the Holy Bible, New International Version®, NIV® Copyright ©1973, 1978, 1984, 2011 by Biblica, Inc.® Used by permission. All rights reserved worldwide.

AMBASSADOR INTERNATIONAL
Emerald House
411 University Ridge, Suite B14
Greenville, SC 29601
United States
www.ambassador-international.com

AMBASSADOR BOOKS
The Mount
2 Woodstock Link
Belfast, BT6 8DD
Northern Ireland, United Kingdom
www.ambassadormedia.co.uk

The colophon is a trademark of Ambassador, a Christian publishing company.

To my husband, George, and my dear friend Gail Bavaird for their unrelenting encouragement that kept me writing.

To my editor, Katie Cruice Smith, who graciously arranged her busy schedule and tirelessly worked to help bring this story to print.

To those who read this book, may you experience the wonderful joy of forgiveness and the happiness that comes from forgiving others.

Chapter 1

Right on time, with her over-sized glasses hanging down on her nose and an over-stuffed briefcase in hand, Natalie arrived at the front door, ready to finalize Charles' schedule for his next piano performance. If ever there was a middle-aged woman of authoritarian appearance, she would take the prize. But regardless of her less-than-attractive appearance, she was a genius at secretarial work and scheduling. She could talk to booking agents and coax them into arranging the best spot for Charles to perform better than Pepper Potts in *Iron Man*. But Natalie was far from ever becoming more than Charles' secretary and booking assistant.

Pushing her glasses up on her nose and ringing the doorbell once more, matronly Sarah opened the door, motioning that she should go directly to Charles' office, which was formerly the library but now a busy office with computers, printers, and papers piled high.

"Natalie, come in," Charles enthusiastically said as he motioned for her to take her usual seat that faced his desk. "Did you finalize everything at the Meyerson Center in Dallas? And oh, did you book my plane ticket?" He knew the answer was yes, but that was a good beginning to get down to work for the next performance.

"I've got everything done; even your overnight suite is all set up at the Ritz-Carlton," said Natalie.

"Great! And I have five days yet to practice. I'll be packing a copy of the Beethoven's Fifth sheet music to take with me. I feel safer should I suddenly go brain dead from fear and need it.

"Now then," he continued, "you know how much I want to perform at the Suntory Hall in Tokyo, Japan. So, what do you think, Natalie? Do I stand a chance at getting booked there? Can you get in touch with someone and get my videos and discs to them?"

Charles' dream for his future was to play at the Musikverein Hall in Austria and the Concertgebouw in Amsterdam. Hard names for even him to pronounce, but an easy and sure route to stardom if he could play in one of those places. An opportunity to play at the famous Suntory Hall in Tokyo would start him on his way.

"I don't think Suntory Hall will be difficult to book a performance," she said, as though it were almost done. "I'll get on that right away so when you get back home from Dallas, you can get working on a new concert performance."

Her confidence in him was overwhelming, but if it wasn't for his magnificent talent at the piano, he would have nothing but grandiose dreams to reach the top. But the truth was that Tokyo and the symphony center were wide open for American performers. Unknowns would be there from all over the U.S.; but the press coverage would be great, and if he did well, he would be labeled as a new world performer. That was part of his plan, and Natalie would do all she could to help.

Working on a new program simply meant taking the many musical works he already knew and rearranging the line-up of their concertos. He played the works of Wolfgang Amadeus Mozart, Ludwig van Beethoven, and Frederic Chopin. These were popular and safe choices for sophisticated audiences packed with lovers of classical music. He enjoyed pop music, too, and included a special treat for his audience by performing a popular song at the end of his program. This was becoming part of his performance signature. He often requested a floor microphone to be at the piano when he reached the end of his classical program, so he could talk to the audience and wittingly introduce the pop song he would sing. This way, he could tie it into a comical line or two and give the audience a special gift that showed his versatility. It was a stratagem that worked. His audience loved it.

******

It was no daydream running through Charles' brain as he sat motionless at the piano while staring out the window of his eighteen-room mansion in Greenwich, Connecticut. Not a daydream or fantasy at all. It was pure nostalgia that caused his fingers to rest reverently upon the keys of his beautiful, shiny, black grand piano. His conscience rebuked him. *How dare you stop practicing.* He had but seven days before he would perform at the magnificent Symphony Hall in Boston. But oh, now his mind was dancing in the revelry of events that had created the wonderful twists and turns of his young life, weaving it into a superlative tale of triumph. What would come next? Dare he continue to dream of performing in Austria or in Amsterdam? Scarcely twenty-four years old and seriously accomplished at the keyboard, Charles truly had an excellent chance to perform in many of the magnificent halls and theaters around the world. His astonishing talent could guarantee this. If he continued working hard at his craft and let his enthusiastic dreams lead the way, he could make it to the top. He could join hands with the rest of the world's most famous pianists.

He let his fingers dance lightly over the keys like the warm-up stretch of an Olympic swimmer who was ready to dive into the water, but he drew back and waited as though lost in wonder, permitting his thoughts to soar into every dream he hoped for.

His love for the piano was owed to his father, Marco, and his talent. Many times, he sat on the bench with him, like an eager boy learning a little ditty and longing to be able to make the piano sing. His father was talented but not gifted enough to pursue a career in music. He was a business genius instead.

Charles' desire for the piano progressed and the call upon his life came as though a summons from Heaven. As his mind went back in time, he remembered that special evening when the call had come. Dinner was over quickly, and they had gathered into the grand room at the penthouse in New York. His father had sat down at the piano, pausing for a moment and then turning to look at him.

"This is my song of praise tonight." His fingers moved with graceful poise over the keys, and he played and sang the most beautiful song his childish heart had ever heard. The melody and words hung in the air, as though they were meant to linger for him alone. So deep, they sank into his heart. *"I do not know just why He came to love me so / He looked beyond my fault and saw my need."*[1] It was then that the cords of his young life were truly stirred. He wanted to learn to play the piano. That was his need.

From that moment on, the world changed. Piano lessons began. His talent grew, astonishing his teachers and family alike. Recitals

---

1   Dottie Rambo, "He Looked Beyond My Fault," *Country Western Hymnal* (Grand Rapids: Singspiration Inc., 1967).

were scheduled. There was no doubt he was truly called into the fine art of music. It was God Almighty Who was pursuing him.

He loved his new Greenwich place, all six acres of it—the beautiful land peppered with linden trees and meticulously manicured. The eighteen-room brick and stone Georgian-style house was set in the most exclusive area of Greenwich. A cobblestone walkway was flanked with full-grown pear trees leading to the door. This place was not plusher and more spacious than the penthouse condominium he grew up in, where his Aunt Ellie and his father still resided. It was Aunt Ellie's penthouse, with a terrace that overlooked New York City and Gramercy Park, still quite beautiful in spite of some deterioration. In the Flatiron District, the happy years of his youth were spent, growing wise and disciplined with his Sicilian father, Marco Ricci, and his American-born mother, Katie.

After his mother's death, Aunt Ellie had become more of a grandmother figure to him, rather than an aunt. She was now the only mother figure in his life. Charles could go to her if he ever needed guidance and godly wisdom. Ties to New York City would never grow dim or become lost. It wasn't so much because of Ellie, but because his father still lived in the penthouse, which remained the family residence. The residence was the gathering place for every birthday, holiday, and client party. His father continued to work at the penthouse office, unless he was needed at the corporate headquarters in the center of Manhattan's business district.

Much of his life was centered in Aunt Ellie's faith and the revered family remembrance of her husband, deceased Uncle Charley. It was old Uncle Charley who had played the main role in the family's fortune. It was Uncle Charley's business savvy that had created the family architect company, which grew into a billion-dollar success. And it was Uncle Charley whom he was named after.

Charles' mind went back to old Uncle Charley, as he sat on the piano bench reminiscing. *I loved that old man,* he thought to himself. *I loved his gruff talk and the stinky cigar that Aunt Ellie complained about. I'd give anything to fly in his corporate jet and have him tell everyone that I am his nephew.*

Charles was fortunate. He was born with a silver spoon in his mouth. And he was blessed that Aunt Ellie's love for her brother was instrumental in giving his father a partnership in the business after Uncle Charley had died.

Things could have gone on forever happy, but the death of his mother brought a void that Charles was hard-pressed to overcome. The sound of her voice and beautiful presence became nothing but a sad, haunting memory. She had left this world much too young and caused the penthouse to become quiet and lonely. The greatest support for his musical career came from her hugs and her smiles as she listened to him practice for hours. She alleged that he played the most beautiful songs she had ever heard.

"Oh, Charles, that was wonderful," she would tell him, even when he missed a note or two and knew he wasn't wonderful.

But she was gone before he completed his advanced studies at Carnegie. Gone, too, was the excitement of her sitting in a theater or grand hall, watching him perform. Though the world was falling in love with him and his performances, his popularity would never be known to her. She would never straighten his tie or brush off his shoulders before he went on stage. She would never see him leave to perform at the gala parties of New York's elite leaders or accompany him to Washington, D.C. to entertain exclusive dignitaries. Without her in the penthouse, he hungered for a place of his own, a place where her memory was not so stark and sorrowful. Greenwich was that place.

Ellie and Marco did their best to coax him to stay in New York, but he was set on moving out. The grandeur of a brilliant career was urging him onward, as well as getting rid of the past that was occupying so much of his heart. He recognized that a brilliant career awaited him, and he needed to leave his past in New York City. The reality of what his life could become repeatedly spurred him on into strict discipline to work hard and get better and better. In his mind, his future was set. His goal was to perform and please the world.

Lightly, he stroked the middle-C key; and just as he did, he was startled by Sarah, who appeared at the archway of the music room.

"Excuse me, Mr. Ricci, but do you want lunch served here or on the garden terrace?"

"Thank you, Sarah," he said, rather surprised. "Here will be fine—and in about an hour if you will bring it to me, please."

"Yes, of course." And with a quick turn, she was gone.

His thoughts carried on as he got up from the piano and walked to the window, thinking back to a time that his memory begged to become real, so he could live again a precious moment spent as a boy in the New York penthouse. As he mused into the past, he thought of a warm evening not too long ago with a cool, summer breeze moving across the terrace, high up on the twenty-fifth floor.

The glow of lights in New York's high-rise buildings sparkled in the darkness, and the sky was lit with hundreds of stars. It was his mother who had started a story—the story of a time before Charles was born.

It began quite reasonably after watching a movie in the theater room that focused on a tale built around a fisherman's wharf. It brought back memories for his mother of Sicily, where his father and Aunt Ellie were born. His mother was reminiscing about the vacation she had spent there.

"I was searching for something," she said to him.

Her best guess about her search was that she still loved his father, though they had not seen each other for months. She had wanted to go to Sicily because Marco had told her many wonderful stories about Catania, a beautiful city by the ocean. His tales were the reason she had traveled there on her own one summer.

So, conversation centered around a movie they had watched that evening that had stirred up lots of nostalgic reminiscing. Charles' mother told the story of her last evening there in Sicily, eating a seafood dinner at the fisherman's wharf. She said it was a dinner that topped all dinners.

The four of them sat eating ice cream on the penthouse terrace in the cool of that star-speckled night, looking out at New York's skyscrapers. He was only a young boy and very much enjoyed his bowl of ice cream and listening to his parents reminisce.

"Remember, Marco? I was dining outside the café in Catania, and you and Ellie walked up."

"Oh, I do remember, darling," his father replied. "I will never forget that evening."

He was listening to them talk but rudely scraping his bowl for the last spoon of ice cream.

"Your father told me all about Catania during the time we knew each other back in Fairview, where I lived before we were married," his mother explained. *"I loved to hear him talk about Sicily and the Roman elements that were still standing after hundreds of years."*

This memory came to him today as if someone had pushed a replay button in his brain. It was sweet and bitter. He turned the wooden window blinds to allow the sun full entrance into the music room. While the blinds were pulled opened, he searched across the landscape, but the view did not distract his thoughts. He was still helpless to stop this memory. He remembered his childish question, coming from a boy of twelve who should have been in bed.

"Were you and Dad dating then?"

"No, we had not seen or talked with each other for a long time, but we still thought about each other. It was shortly after Jake passed away."

Charles knew about Jake, all right. He was his mother's first husband who had died after a motorcycle accident.

"So, there I was eating my dinner," his mother told him. *"And suddenly, I see your father and Aunt Ellie walking toward me. Neither of us knew the other was vacationing in Sicily. But Aunt Ellie had a premonition of some sort that was urging her to make that trip, and she talked your father into going with her. They spotted me and walked to my table. I invited them to sit down; and as it turned out, we had dinner together. Right after that, we started dating."*

Charles was stunned, thinking that they had run into each other thousands of miles away from home. Aunt Ellie was barely able to contain herself from talking about it.

"Well, it wasn't strange that they found each other; it was the Lord working His plan," she said. "God knew all along that your father and mother were to be together, and that's how He worked it out."

He thought many times later that it was a miracle for his parents to meet each other again, far across the ocean, thousands of miles from home. It seemed like finding a needle in a haystack. Aunt Ellie was right when she said it was an unexplained phenomenon of God's intervention.

That same night on the terrace, Marco suggested they all visit Catania, Sicily.

Breaking his thoughts, Sarah brought in a tray carrying a sandwich piled high of deli-sliced ham and a chilled can of Coke sitting beside it.

"Would there be anything else?" she questioned, as Charles moved away from the window.

"No, that's fine. Put the lunch here on the table next to this chair," he directed. "Oh, and tomorrow when Natalie comes, we will be spending a long time going over my schedules. She'll be staying for lunch, so if you would be so kind, I'd like to have your delicious chicken salad stuffed into fresh croissants." Then he added, "We'll eat in the terrace garden."

She smiled and said, "I'll be happy to make chicken salad because I know Natalie loves that sandwich." Then she said to him with a big grin, "You're always so pleasingly demanding. There's perfection in every detail of your life, right down to where lunch should be served and what should be eaten. You know, Charles, I'm old enough to be your grandmother, and that makes me love you and enjoy working for you."

"Thank you, Sarah," Charles said, not willing to show his own affection for his elderly housekeeper.

And why shouldn't she love him? Her quarters were in a beautiful, small studio apartment at the back part of the mansion. She was thankful for the work that offered room and board along with a small salary. Sixty-seven years old and thankful to be healthy enough to manage the job with the help of a younger weekly maid who came to do the heavy cleaning.

After Sarah had left the room, Charles sat down, knowing that when he finished eating, he must get back to the piano. He snapped the Coke can open and avoided pouring the drink into the glass. He took a sip from the can and found his nostalgia still teasing his thoughts once more. That trip to Catania was an important highlight in his life. His father had treated him as though he were a young lion. He could still sense how his twelve-year-old heart was feeling the connection to his roots. His cell phone camera had captured it all. Those pictures were carefully saved in his computer and later printed and put into a photo album, yet he had not looked at them for years.

While he ate the sandwich and washed it down with the Coke, his mind went back to Catania and the visit to his grandparents' graves before they had returned home to New York. It was a hallowed visit, and he remembered how much his father wished his parents could know him.

"I wish your grandmother and grandfather were here to see you," Marco said to him. They were standing at the Ricci headstone, and like any twelve-year-old child, Charles asked his father if his grandparents knew they were there.

"I don't know, son, but if you think they are here, then you should believe they are."

He finished the sandwich and grabbed the unfinished Coke, taking it with him to the window again. Looking across the courtyard and down to the sandy beach of Long Island Sound, only yards from his front door, he wished it could lead to a beautiful woman with whom he would share his deepest thoughts and love.

Oh, for his own sake, he needed to stop this insane, melancholy wistfulness. But seeing the sun trickling through the linden trees brought back again the cemetery scene in Catania. It was strange that day—how the sky was covered with clouds all day, but suddenly the sun popped out as if it were an omen of God shining upon the graves.

Charles smiled as he remembered what he had said to Aunt Ellie.

"I'll bet Grandfather and Grandmother are happy to see me here."

"Indeed, they are happy, Charlie."

The concert at the Symphony Hall in Boston was a huge success. The audience would not let him leave. After a marvelous standing ovation, the bravos and clapping continued while flowers were tossed onto the stage. Finally, after two additional popular songs, he bowed for the last time and walked off the stage. Marco and Ellie quickly made their way backstage to congratulate him.

"Son, it was superb," Marco said, giving him a bear hug.

"Thanks, Dad."

One might think he would say something curt or funny to his father in an effort to brush off the tension he was hiding after striking thousands of notes without a mistake. But he was basically happy it was over, and his performance was self-gratifying. He was always aware, maybe even tormented, that there would be one perfectly pitched person in the audience who would know in a flash if he missed a note. Tonight, however, his performance was perfect.

No matter how far his father and Ellie had to travel or how many meetings Marco had to reschedule, they would be in his audience, supporting him. Both knew that he was on his way to stardom, and their support was paramount to his success. Natalie booked their tickets and plane reservations on the same day she booked Charles'. If it meant a stay-over, they spent the night in the same hotel. Once or twice, Marco transported all of them on the company jet, bringing them back home in the wee hours of the morning. The contracted pilot was always willing to accommodate them. No one thought much of this luxury because it came routinely and expected. They lived in a world of privilege. Yet they were the few rich who were able to go through the camel's needle and remain dedicated to God.

Charles' strong arms cut through the cool water with each stroke. He swam almost every day for exercise, and his body felt stronger with each lap. He had helped design this beautiful pool with the help of his architect father. The impressive Caribbean blue surfacing under the rippling water was Marco's suggestion. The tiles surrounding the pool were imported from the Middle East and were a custom pattern of hand-painted Mediterranean blues and corals worked into a white background. It had taken ten months to complete this project, and rarely did he miss a day to swim.

He was getting out of the pool when Sarah came to tell him Natalie was on the phone.

"She knows you're in the pool and said she would wait for you to dry off."

Sarah laid the phone down on a poolside table and left.

Charles grabbed a towel and hastily picked up the phone.

"What's up, Natalie?" he said, still drying his legs.

"I just got word from the Suntory Hall in Tokyo that another performer will be on stage before you go on. It's a female soprano singer named Abigail Clark. She's not well-known—new on the scene—but Tokyo is giving her a chance."

"So, they're using me as the draw, huh? Is that it?"

Charles was taken aback, but if he was slated after the soprano, the audience automatically knew that he was the cream of the crop and saved for last.

"Charles," Natalie continued, "they sent a YouTube address of one of her performances. I opened it. She's good, and she's beautiful. I've forwarded the message to you."

"Okay. I'll look at it, but at this late date into the schedule, I don't want to put up a fuss about sharing the stage. I just hope the press is kinder to me than her." He said this with a sarcastic chuckle, exposing his besetting sin of arrogance and pride.

That evening, after Sarah was finished in the kitchen and went to her quarters, he poured a glass of flavored water and took it into the library. Sitting comfortably at his desk, he opened Natalie's message and clicked on the YouTube download. To his surprise, the first picture and sound were that of a full symphony orchestra. The camera then focused on Abigail, standing in front of a microphone, in a floor-length, aqua blue gown that draped slightly off her shoulders. She began to sing as the camera moved in close to her face. Charles sat there in shock. She was beautiful. Her voice was clear and wonderful.

Who is this Abigail Clark? he thought. *Why haven't I heard of her?* He listened and actually felt moved.

The next morning, he called Natalie.

"I'm okay with this singer Abigail Clark sharing the stage before my performance," he told her. "Call Tokyo and tell them it's okay but emphasize that I expect the same payment, no dividing, and let them know I want good press."

"Got it," Natalie affirmed. Then she added, "Send me your concert program; they've asked for it. The orchestra needs it pronto."

It was all set. Natalie and his little family of Marco and Aunt Ellie would travel with him to Tokyo and trust that God was opening the door to bigger and better things. This would be his first performance in a foreign country, and visibility of this type would entice sought-after performances.

During the few days before the Tokyo concert, he practiced faithfully. Sharing the stage with someone else created greater force to be more than just flawless. Several times before turning out the lights and going to bed, he went into the library and watched the YouTube video of Abigail Clark. His better judgment cautioned him. *Forget it, Charlie; she's too beautiful and gifted for you.*

Chapter 2

Four pairs of eyes blinked in unison as they focused on the sight that was far more beautiful in person than the photos they saw at home. It was an awesome, breathtaking moment for Charles and his small group when they walked into the Suntory Hall for a quick peek after landing at Tokyo's Narita International Airport. The architect and the sounding in the hall showcased world-class genius. Charles was like a tourist who was taking in the sight of the Grand Canyon for the first time. The stage he would perform on seemed like a throne fit for a king. And Marco, with his architectural knowledge, was speechless thinking how fantastic it would be to supervise the construction of a magnificent structure like this.

The main hall was designed in a vineyard-style, the first of its type in Japan. Charles' eyes made a slow, panoramic sweep of the two thousand seats surrounding the stage, remembering that all grapevine terraces are orientated toward the sun. This was the concept here.

Anxious jitters were starting to crawl all over him now that he was in Tokyo, but they were not caused by the pangs of early stage fright. They were the nervous butterflies of meeting Abigail Clark.

After finishing a quick view of the hall, a Japanese attendant transported them to their hotel. Charles needed to swallow a bite to eat and change clothes before returning to the hall to meet with Abigail, the conductor, and the director. He knew enough not to dress like he was attending a prim-and-starchy event but desired to come off as a slick professional, maybe even a bit star-like. He chose a semi-shiny, crepe-like, white shirt with rolled up sleeves atop a pair of dark navy designer jeans. Casual shoes that mimicked sandals made him look as though he belonged to the elite of Tokyo.

As the attendant slowed the car to a halt outside the hall, Charles smoothed his hair and took a deep breath. Another attendant opened the door of the van. Charles grabbed his satchel and started toward the main doors. Already on stage was the conductor, David Lewzinski. Standing with him was a female. Charles took a wild but accurate guess that she was Abigail Clark.

The walk down the long aisle to the stage seemed like walking the length of a football field. Viewing Lewzinski from afar, it appeared he resembled the famous Toscanini, with gray, curly hair and a dark mustache. A truly distinguished appearance that made Charles feel as though he was diving in far above his head, yet knowing that this was a chance of a lifetime, forced him to shake off the nervous jitters. His eyes met Abigail's as he climbed the stage stairs and reached the group. She stared at him and then broke it off quickly.

"Charles Ricci, this is Conductor David Lewzinski," the director said. They shook hands and exchanged a warm, expected greeting.

Then turning to Abigail, who was dressed in a stunning, white, three-piece pant suit the director introduced the two performers.

"Charles Ricci, this is Soprano Abigail Clark."

Awed by Abigail's beautiful face, which was framed by straight, black hair, Charles reached out his hand and gave a warm and polite greeting, abandoning his arrogance that he was last on the program and was considered the big draw.

With introductions made, the business of finalizing the program got underway, first with the stage lighting and then the conductor asking questions. He would work separately with each of them before nightfall, rehearsing with the full orchestra on stage. This was the critical time both conductor and performer would learn each other's styles and their commanding influences, which was key to a smooth and lyrical performance.

"It's a great piano selection you made, Mr Ricci," Lewzinski commented. "We will have your piano on stage quickly. Take a breather now while the stage is being set up and the orchestra takes their seats."

This organized leadership meant Lewzinski would work with Charles first. An honored gesture, showing respect likely attributed to Charles' popularity in the U.S. and also due to his stalwart choice of a Steinway & Sons grand Tokyo piano. Few pianists would select this grand from the collection offered him, but Charles had a keen observation of the hall's size and knew he needed the best sound possible. His selection was the grand model with African, pommeled finish. Charles' quality and perfection impressed Lewzinski.

Abigail and Charles walked off the stage together. Taking the lead to get acquainted, he suggested they walk throughout the center and view the smaller hall.

"I would love to do that," Abigail said, smiling.

While they walked toward the small hall, Abigail asked if he knew the story of the hall and that it was named the Blue Rose.

"No, I did not know that," Charles answered, feeling more comfortable that she was initiating conversation.

He could not help noticing how very attractive she was and how crazy his mind was wondering, like how he would get to see her again after their performance. He was way ahead of the game in his imagination, but he had a lot of Aunt Ellie in him, and nothing was impossible.

Abigail took the opportunity to tell him that she had researched the hall and found some interesting facts.

"Well, you know now that the small hall is referred to as the Blue Rose," she said, looking at him to determine if he was interested in knowing more.

"Ah, yes. Obviously, the blue color is for a special reason."

"Yes, and it's quite interesting," she said while they stepped into the hall. "The term 'blue rose' is regarded as a synonym for something that is impossible to have or to achieve. Blue roses are considered impossible to create, but Suntory biomechanically created one of a special blue hue several years ago. The small hall was renamed Blue Rose in the hope that artists would use it to stage their impossible challenges."

By now, they were fully inside the Blue Rose Hall and taking in the architecture.

Abigail continued, "Wood was used extensively so that the sound in here would be warm and create a cozier atmosphere. It's a type of setting where one feels closer to the performers. Did you know that the seating is movable?"

Charles was beginning to feel as though he was taking a course called Blue Rose 101 with all the teachable facts Abigail was sharing.

"No, I didn't know that," he admitted, hoping she would continue talking because he was too engrossed with her sparkling personality to think of anything to discuss.

Abigail jumped right in. "Yes, all of it is movable and can be used imaginatively to create new types of musical spaces. I don't know exactly how the spaces would be arranged, but I guess a cello performer would desire a certain type of seating, as would a harpist."

"That's just amazing," Charles said, turning so they could walk back to the main hall.

Amazing was right. He saw she was not solely beautiful and talented but knowledgeable as well. Not at all like some of the flighty clients whom his father often entertained. He liked her, and it caused him to feel somewhat nervous, maybe even intimidated. He struggled for something to talk about while they walked toward the main hall. He could hear the orchestra tuning up. Suddenly, he had a flash race through his brain. *Oh my, she will hear me play in just a moment.*

"I see you are from Bar Harbor, Maine," he managed to get out. "That's a beautiful place. Do you live on the ocean side?"

He blurted this out as though he had to get all his comments and questions in at the same time. At this moment, they were entering the main hall, and the orchestra sounded like a thousand instruments chatting with each other.

"Yes, I live in Bar Harbor," she answered. "And yes, I live near the ocean side."

That was all the time left to talk. The conductor was motioning for Charles. The grand piano was center stage, and the spotlights were adjusted to what Charles and the director thought was perfect. The spotlight beaming down on the piano created an image as though it were a sleeping giant, waiting to be awakened. Charles turned to Abigail as if to excuse himself, and she smiled and said, "Break a leg." They both burst into laughter. That spoken cliché was a gift that came just at the right moment to calm and settle him down. He turned from her and took the stage.

Comfortably seating himself on the bench, he began feeling right at home, like a guest in someone's house who had just offered him their finest wine. He took a moment to slightly bow his head toward the keys in an effort to bring his spirit and soul into subjection, as though he awaited the anointing of God.

All spotlights were on. Lewzinski, now ready with arms stretched in the upward poise and baton in his right hand and the left hand open, he turned just enough to await Charles' cue that he was ready to play.

The music captured every space in the hall. The acoustic response of the sounds bouncing back and forth from the walls and down from the ceiling was magnificent. The notes Charles played were pure and crystal clear.

Lewzinski was captivated. As soon as the run-through was completed, he walked to the piano and offered a handshake. "Superlative."

"Thank you, sir. The pleasure is all mine."

Charles was very pleased with his performance, and like all artists, he evaluated himself with the most critical authority. To be pleased was a good thing. But if there was credit due, it belonged to God.

Abigail was up on stage before Charles exited. "Charles, that was simply wonderful," she said to him. "I have to admit, though, that your talent makes me a bit self-conscious if you stay for my rehearsal. But I would be honored if you would stay."

Would he stay? Wild horses wouldn't drag him off to the hotel. After all, he wanted to hear her in the flesh. But most of all, he wanted to show that he was definitely interested in her performance.

Conductor Lewzinski waited for Abigail to position herself at the microphone that stood next to the piano. She nodded, and the orchestra began to play. The first song was from the musical *Evita*—"Don't Cry for Me Argentina." The next song, "Summertime," was from the movie *Porgy and Bess*. Nothing classical, which amazed Charles, as she sang two more songs that were crowd-pleasers but not classical.

He was spellbound. Abigail's voice was pure and without even a hint of rasp when hitting high notes. He understood why Suntory Hall would book her. His arrogant attitude at home about the press being kinder to him than her was scrapped immediately. Her talent was superior. Perhaps on a higher plane than his.

They parted the hall and wished each other luck for tomorrow's performance.

Back at the hotel, though it was late, Charles could not stop talking about the dignity of Conductor Lewzinski and the perfect precision of him and the orchestra.

"He was so gracious. He made me feel as though he was subservient to me, which I believe I could never stand on equal ground with him."

Natalie was beaming with joy listening to his accelerating enthusiasm. He went on and on about the sound that radiated off of every wall.

"The resonance simply exploded in the air when the orchestra started. I can't tell you how I felt as I touched the keys and heard them literally burst forth from every space in that hall."

Ellie interrupted his nonstop chatter.

"I can't wait to hear you tomorrow. Now, what about that soprano? What was her name?"

Charles deliberately choked up and went over to the bar, poured a glass of soda, and started up again.

"Abigail. That's her name. She has the most beautiful soprano voice. Truly, she may be the draw for the audience, not me." Charles said this without exhibiting any guile and then drank down the soda as though he were dry as a desert.

Natalie acknowledged that Abigail was not only talented but also beautiful, remembering the video she had watched of her back home. She glanced at Charles to catch an expression but got nothing. He was too smart to take the bait. Above all, he played it coy because if Aunt Ellie got wind of any attraction, she would start an exhortation about fate and holy Providence. Charles knew better about sudden attractions. During his college years, he had developed a friendly relationship with another music major and realized that beauty and talent are not wrapped up in goodness. Before getting too close to this classmate, he discovered that she was drenched in New Age philosophy, and her god was herself. There was much to learn about Abigail before he would ever allow himself to become close friends.

Marco looked at his watch, noticing that it was almost midnight.

"We better call it a night and go to bed. How about we meet in the dining room downstairs for breakfast at nine?"

The suggestion was well-taken. Natalie and Ellie went to their rooms, and the night ended on an exciting note of high expectation for Charles.

The next morning, Charles stayed at the hotel while the rest went off sightseeing with a hired guide, eager to show them the interesting areas of Tokyo. The man was very slight and exhibited a meek style that most Japanese attendants expose. He performed the proper bows and gestures for the anticipated tip.

Charles sat at the edge of a plush, upholstered chair staring down at his music sheets spread out on the carpet in front of him. He concentrated on every printed note as though he were playing each one. It seemed that his career depended on the kind of artistic expression and perfection he needed to please both the audience and the press. He knew if he allowed the weight of anxious expectation to get hold of him, he would not perform flawlessly.

"God," he whispered softly, "You said I can do all things through You. I need Your help tonight. I can't do this without Your help."

The hour came quickly when everyone was impeccably dressed and ready to board the van transporting them to the Suntory Hall. The family opted to go early with Charles to avoid any confusion or delays.

Charles was dressed in a white button-down shirt, black slacks, and a black waistcoat. He chose to wear a colorful cummerbund, feeling that the audience was a sophisticated collection who appreciated elegance. His jacket was tailored to give him full mobility while not being too baggy. During the popular song he planned to play at the end of his performance, he would stand and take the jacket off, roll up his sleeves, and situate himself at the piano again. He had these maneuvers staged in his mind. Then he planned to look at the audience with a smile and give them his signature mark—a song the whole world would know.

The Suntory Hall was packed. All two thousand seats held a person anxious to hear tonight's performance. Abigail's parents were seated in the audience, unknown to Charles' family. Marco, Ellie, and Natalie were seated front row and scanning the program sheet.

The curtain lifted, and the orchestra and conductor stayed quiet while Abigail Clark walked on stage, dressed in a light blue, loosely flowing pantsuit. The audience broke out into applause. She gave a gracious wave and took her position near the piano. The pop songs were well-received with whistling and clapping, even a few hoots and howls. The orchestra played while she left the stage. Two female attendants quickly helped her out of the pantsuit and into a bright red gown that sat snuggly at the edge of each shoulder and traveled down into a V. Her hair was rapidly arranged with one side drawn back behind her shoulder, the other crimped beautifully about her face. She walked back on stage. Enthusiastic applause broke out. Charles was watching from a distance behind the curtains.

Taking her position at the marked spot in the middle of the stage, she waited for Lewzinski to command the orchestra to begin. Every ear waited.

Softly, the orchestra began. Abigail waited for the cue note and then began to sing "O Mio Babbina Caro." The audience stayed respectfully silent as the beautiful aria filled the hall. Ellie was brought to tears. Marco and Natalie were noticeably moved. At the end of the song, the audience gave her a noisy standing ovation while a Japanese attendant brought her a bouquet of roses and bowed gracefully. Abigail bowed again to the audience and walked off stage. The audience continued to clap unstoppably. She returned and blew a kiss in all directions while putting her right hand over her heart. She left the stage and was immediately met by her parents.

"Wonderful performance," her father told her as he gathered her into his arms. Without hesitation, her mother pushed her way in.

"It was beautiful, sweetheart," she told her.

Charles questioned himself in a rare moment of intimidation. *How in the world can I follow such a performance?* But then he reminded himself that she was like the warmup act that a star often demands before going on stage. The great passion the audience gave for "O Mio Babbina Caro" would certainly be expressed with his rendition of Beethoven's Fifth.

The curtain went down as the prized piano was brought to the center of the stage. Charles stood off-stage, barely out of sight as the curtain opened and the spotlights slowly illuminated the orchestra and the piano. He entered the stage. Two thousand pairs of hands applauded while he walked to the piano. Immediately, he sensed he had a generous following seated in the audience. Some no doubt had flown from different parts of the U.S. and England. There was something unique and wonderful about their enthusiastic clapping. It was like the icing on the cake or the kiss of your mother when she's proud of you. Oh, how he wished Katie were there to watch and hear him play.

He gracefully acknowledged the audience and took his seat at the piano. Lewzinski watched carefully as Charles seated himself on the bench. The orchestra begin to play. Charles sat still, waiting for his part to begin playing. His hands were placed at his lap, and then he brought them into position. With great ease and eloquence, he began to play. The walls of the hall resounded perfectly with every note crystal clear.

It would mean so much to Charles to truly know if Katie could see her son on that enormous stage. The twelve-year-old heart still living within him was hopeful for the possibility that she was watching him and following his life.

******

Ellie sat as if she was perched on a pin cushion. She continually interrupted her listening ear to silently pray. *No mistakes, God, please.* If she wasn't praying, she was inconspicuously watching the reaction of those sitting around her. Marco was calm, and like any proud father, he was basking in the pride of his son, the maestro, performing before an audience of two thousand people. He would continue to do all in his power to see him reach his dream and reach the top. Natalie sat as though she knew her boss would hallmark this booking and it would be the final step into a worldwide-calling to perform in the greatest of halls and theaters of the world. She knew his dedication and persistent discipline would pay off. There wasn't one worry that he would perform perfectly.

And that he did.

Just as expected, the audience loved both the classical and the signature pop at the end. Demanding that he play again, he returned to the stage and gave them the biggest surprise of all. He lowered the microphone to the same level as his chin. The audience sat quiet and waiting. He began playing "Someone You Loved"—the song made popular by Lewis Capaldi. Tonight, it was Charles Ricci who sang the song.

The astonished audience cheered as they began to identify the song and recognize that Charles had stepped out of the classical and into true pop. Marco and Ellie turned and stared at each other, their mouths open. Natalie just cringed down into her chair and wondered what in the world he was thinking to do that. But the twist he gave the song was so smooth and tasteful that it was more like warm topping trickling down over the main part of the treat. The lyrics almost like an unknown, unrecognized plea for the woman of his dreams. *I need somebody to heal / Somebody to know / Somebody to have / Somebody to hold / It's easy to say . . . "*[2] He let the piano keys finish the song and then moved the microphone aside so he could stand up. The audience stood up with him. Clapping and whistling. It was almost outrageous how his performance was ending with a second standing ovation.

******

Charles smiled from ear to ear. *Are you watching this, Mom? I can't believe how much they love me, and it's all because of you and God.*

Back at the hotel, Marco had settled himself down and was ecstatically pleased and bubbling with pride that Charles was so inventive with his program. He could not deny that the audience loved the pop overture.

"Your brilliance amazes me, Charlie," he said, using the family nickname.

Ellie burst in. "Yes, but be careful that the type of career you want doesn't get away from you by spoofing the audience with pop, even if they do like it."

She was right. Charles was talented enough to have either career. But what he truly loved and desired to play was the timeless and unforgettable music that true lovers of the fine arts appreciate.

"Well, I think it was genius that you played and sang that song," Natalie broke in. "At first, I couldn't believe you had chosen such a song. But the way you played it . . . The press will take that surprising

---

2   Lewis Capaldi, "Someone You Loved," *Someone You Loved*, Vertigo Berlin, No. 1, 2019, CD.

curve and headline it to your good. You watch; tomorrow, the press will make the public salivate to see and hear you again.

Charles was drained and collapsed onto the bed after everyone went off to their own quarters. Staring into the semi-darkness of his room, brightened by light coming through the drapes, he recognized that Tokyo was much like New York City, always lit and never sleeping. His mind went over his concert piece by piece and then onto Abigail's starlit performance. He knew very little about her, except that she was someone he wanted to get to know better.

There was just seven-and-a-half hours before he would be packed and transported with his family into the heart of Tokyo and the business area for a special luncheon that Suntory was hosting as a farewell brunch for Charles and Abigail. This was the proper departure for all American performers and the custom of Suntory's executives. Special food preparations were being provided at Chiasa's Shinjuku, one of the most elite and expensive restaurants in Tokyo. Charles' hopes were high that this luncheon would lend an excellent opportunity for him to get to know Abigail better.

The wakeup call came much too soon, but Charles and his family arrived on time at the restaurant and were awaiting their seating arrangements when Abigail and her parents arrived. Suntory executives were already there, and Japanese attendants stood waiting to serve. The Riccis and Natalie met Abigail and her parents, Rob and Irene Clark, before being seated.

If Ellie could speak her opinioned mind, she would insist that it was not mere coincidence that Abigail and Charles were seated next to each other. To her, it would be Providence. But her assumption would be wrong. Protocol in the affluent musical arena of Japan automatically placed the performers together at the departing breakfast.

The atmosphere was dazzling. The servers were in traditional Geisha attire, strictly for Japanese effect and flamboyance. Sake— the traditional sweet Japanese rice wine—was offered, but Charles refused it, preferring to drink tea. Dessert was a dish of ice cream with small mochi rice dumplings called Shiratuma. Charles tasted every food offered to him, but if he were asked, he would prefer Manhattan-style pizza and Coney Island hot dogs.

Conversations were light and polite, except for Abigail and Charles. They took up where they left off during rehearsal at the Suntory Hall, even discussing their career goals.

"Do you have a busy schedule once you get back home?" Charles asked her, hoping to find out more about her.

"Just enough to keep me busy. How about you?" She quickly added, "If you're like me, you're hoping for a big invitation that will give your career a huge break."

He sipped his tea and set the cup back onto the table, turning toward her.

"Oh, you've got that right. I'm looking for the invitations that will move me up to the big theaters worldwide. I would love to play in Europe at the historical theaters." He chuckled a little as he spoke, to ward off any suspicion that he was hungry for great success.

She nodded, letting him know that her dream was the same. Their conversation became comfortable at that point. They ate and chatted as though they were good friends.

Marco and Ellie made occasional small talk with Abigail's parents, who sat across the table from them.

"Your daughter's voice is beautiful," Marco said to Rod, stressing the word *beautiful* and hoping to start up a conversation.

Yes, thank you," Rod said with a proud grin. "She has worked hard to build a career. We're very proud of her."

Their talk drifted on with polite conversations about unimportant matters that did not lead to any great sense of camaraderie. But just as well, for this trip belonged to Charles and Abigail.

Before ending the breakfast, Charles took the nerve to ask for Abigail's cell number and was happily surprised that she gave it to him and requested his as well.

While the van drove them to the airport, Charles was quiet, as though he had enough stimulus to last for months. In lieu of the whole experience, he was silently contemplating that this trip and his performance might be very fortunate for two reasons. One, he was sure that other engagements would be offered to him. Second, he had been petitioning God for a woman he could share his deepest thoughts and love with. Maybe he had found her.

Chapter 3

A few lengths in the swimming pool and some of Sarah's good cooking and Charles was as happy and rested as a house sparrow taking up residence in a thick, green arborvitae. Natalie, however, was busy with her boss' career and working full speed to lock in his next booking. She was quite the nag, meeting often with him to discuss the invitations he was getting at various theaters and halls.

"Time never stops, Charles," she said, looking seriously at him. "When the water is warm, you have to jump in. Remember, theaters do their booking far in advance. You can't wait too long. The invitations you are getting now will soon be closed."

There wasn't a lazy bone in Charles' body, but he was wasting time daydreaming about Abigail. Should he call her? Should he search for her schedule of performances and attend one? Secretly, he was keeping these thoughts and emotions to himself, feeling uncomfortable about how he felt. Abigail was different than any other girl he had met. In the two days he was with her, he liked everything about her. She had class, and she would fit into his life perfectly. At least, he thought so, if she was a Christian. Crazy, how the love bug makes everything seem perfect. But he didn't know her. All he knew was that Abigail Clark was a beautiful soprano, new to the world of entertainment, and that she lived in Bar Harbor, Maine, near the ocean, which seemed to indicate she was from a rich family like him. And both of them being accomplished artists in the field of music, she seemed to fit.

Natalie was pushing him, and he could feel the pressure, even in his daydreaming. His fixations about Abigail had to wait. Performing again soon was what he needed to do.

"Okay, give me a list of invitations and the dates," he said to Natalie.

He was agreeable with Natalie that his next performance should be in California. The invitation to the Wiltern Theater was the result of good press coming from his concert at the Suntory Hall in Tokyo. The Wiltern was one of the best choices for him to get visibility and press in this uncharted area. It held seating well over a thousand. Considering that it was the largest auditorium in Los Angeles and showcased a period of elegance not found anywhere in modern venues, it was a perfect choice for him. Photos of it were extremely convincing. The entrance picture showed the building set back with colorful terrazzo paving clear to the street. The art deco inside pictured unusual tile patterns and fascinating murals. The most dramatic element of the entire theater was the sunburst design on the ceiling of the auditorium.

"This will be great," he said to Natalie as they scanned the remainder of the photos. "Get back with them and confer that the payment is acceptable, but haggle a little to get the flight there and back paid by them, as well as paying for the hotel room." This was just good business to Charles.

"I want two nights so I'm not exhausted having to board a red eye flight back. Get what you can, but don't let the offer get away."

It was all set. Charles would perform at the Wiltern in less than two weeks, and Natalie would continue to book other theaters and halls to assure he had at least sixteen months of engagements with several weeks rest in between. From that point on, it would be no problem for him to perform whenever he chose. Truly, the Suntory performance launched his career, and he was in high spirits being sought after. Yet his heart still hoped that one day, he would get an invitation to perform in Vienna, Austria, at the Muskverein Hall and the Netherlands at the Royal Concertgebouw Theater in Amsterdam.

He hardly had time to think about Abigail with his busy schedule, but her memory came to him off and on. He wondered how her performance schedule was progressing, and he prodded his imagination to assume that she might still think about him.

At this point in Charles' life, the question could be asked which to believe—the power of Providence or the luck of good fortune—because while Natalie was searching theater bookings, she came across a brochure advertising Abigail Clark performing at Carnegie Hall in just two weeks. Casually, she mentioned it to Charles.

"Get me a ticket," he said to her. "I want to see Abigail again."

Natalie jumped back in surprise, a bit puzzled at Charles' eagerness, but she had no clue that he was still thinking about her.

"If you can get a ticket at this late date, I'm going to call her and let her know I'll be in the audience. I'll drive to New York and stay at the penthouse with Dad and Aunt Ellie. I just might take her to dinner," he said with a spark in his voice.

Charles was sitting on top of the world with this shipshape plan to call Abigail and try to drum up a visit with her. He still had her cell number in his data file, and she was listed in his Google contacts. If Natalie could get a ticket, he would call Abigail tonight after dinner. If she accepted, he would call his father and let him know he'd be staying in his abandoned bedroom at the penthouse for the weekend and plead to hold Aunt Ellie off from projecting anything other than a friendly connection with Abigail. If by chance, Abigail had another day before going back to Bar Harbor, he would invite her to the penthouse.

Taking a cup of coffee with him into his music room, he sat down at the computer and pulled up Abigail's phone number. All she could do was say no. Nothing to lose, everything to gain. He took a sip of coffee and called her.

"Hello, is this Abigail?"

"Yes! Hi, Charles. I caught your name on my screen. How are you?" her voice was cheerful.

"I'm good. How about you?"

The conversation opened up wide. Abigail told him things were good but didn't mention she would be performing at Carnegie Hall. It was up to him to bring this to attention and suggest what was on his mind.

"Well, I see you have a performance coming up soon at Carnegie Hall."

He waited for her to respond.

"Yes. I'm performing in the main hall again. I'm really excited."

This was his cue to let her know he was coming to New York City and that he would be in the audience.

"I'm visiting my father in New York that weekend. I saw an advertisement about your performance, and I bought a ticket."

He waited for her to respond.

"Well, that's wonderful," she said laughing. "At least I know I'll have one person in the audience. Maybe we can find a chance to chat."

She swung the door wide open for him, and he walked right in.

"Absolutely," he affirmed. "I'm thinking that your performance is early enough that we can go for dinner afterward." Then without hesitating, he added, "Do you have a layover?"

Abigail responded affirmatively to both. Yes for dinner and yes her flight back home wasn't until the next evening.

"Great," he said, like someone who had just won the lottery.

"I'll make reservations for dinner, and if you don't have anything planned the next day, I'd like very much for you to join my family for lunch at their place. They live in the Gramercy Park area. I know they would love to see you again."

Then he quickly added, "It will just be the two of us and my father and Aunt Ellie."

The few seconds waiting for her to respond seemed like an eternity filled with nos.

"Well, I would like that very much. I originally planned to spend the time shopping the next day, but lunch sounds much better. And it would be wonderful to see your father and your aunt again."

They finished their chat, and it was all set. Charles leaned back in his office chair, putting his hands behind his head and staring at the ceiling amazed. Just a few hours ago, Abigail was far from any of his thoughts, but now his mind was again swimming with her. He grabbed the phone and called his father.

"Well, that's great," Marco said. "Can't think of a better way to spend a weekend."

"It should be a great weekend. Do me a favor; talk to Aunt Ellie," Charles said sternly. "I don't want her getting all excited. You know how she is. I don't want her to make Abigail uncomfortable."

"Relax, Charles," his dad said, perturbed.

Yet both of them knew Ellie could get excited over something as trivial as finding a vacant parking place at the Times Square Parking Garage. It never just happened. It had to be God Who opened it up just for her. Neither of them doubted her passion nor her faith about every detail concerning life, but on many occasions, she carried things too far. Besides, Charles was doing nothing but testing the water. If it wasn't right, he would back away.

******

Ironically, Charles did not know that Abigail had the same feelings about him—that she, too, was lonely and hoping to someday find someone to share her life with. She had left Japan with a crush on him, and it was still holding a year and a half later. His talent, his personality, the way he was easy to talk to—everything about him left her wanting to get to know him better. But she knew it was best to keep pushing his memory from her mind. The career she was working toward was the most important thing in her life, and there was no room for romance. She loved singing as much as Charles loved playing the piano.

Carnegie Hall was no new place to Abigail. The only difference this time was that she would enjoy a sold-out audience. Her customary program was all pop music, mostly ballads. Occasionally, she did something classical but very soft and along the line of "Ave Maria" or the Italian ballad "Because We Believe." Lately, it appeared that her audience wanted more classical, so she was working on introducing one or two at each performance. She played to an exceedingly diverse crowd that gave her freedom to experiment, and hopefully, Charles would become one of her diverse fans.

******

Pulling into the Whittier parking garage, Charles felt a stab at his heart while a thousand memories suddenly came alive. There was no shrugging them off. He still missed the place where he grew up. Stepping off the elevator on the twenty-fifth floor and walking into the penthouse stirred up mixed emotions of nostalgia. No one forgets their happy childhood or manages to smother the sadness of losing a parent. He doubted he would ever forget his mother, no matter how happy life might become for him.

Marco was standing in the outer hallway when the elevator doors opened.

"Hey, son!" he said, grabbing the overnight bag and slipping his arm around his shoulder.

"Hi, Dad. I see you got that new sport car parked in the Ricci parking slot." He was laughing because he knew how much his father wanted that car and how much a kid his dad still was.

"Man! That set of tires can really go," Marco said, laughing with him. "We'll take it for a spin later on."

It was good to be back home and shaking off some of the seclusion of his Greenwich place. New York would always stay in his blood, and the penthouse would remain as cozy as a cottage on a quiet lake. And he found things were just as they were during his last visit two months ago. Funny how Ellie never changed anything. Every visit he made found the place consistent and unaffected. But nothing needed to be changed. The penthouse was beautifully decorated and furnished with plush chairs and couches and ornate tables in Louis XIV-style. It depicted the Riccis' stylish and graceful preferences. Every piece of furniture in the grand room was shipped from England. Paintings and tapestries, gold lamps, carved statues, and plush carpets gave the high-rise condominium the look of a luxury gallery. The twelve-hundred-square-foot terrace, overlooking Gramercy Park, was perfect for parties and luncheons and just sitting and talking.

"Hey there, Aunt Ellie," he said walking into the kitchen where he found her putting icing on a cake.

"Charlie!" she squealed. "Get over here and let me hug you." She wiped her hands quickly and grabbed hold of him. Then came that special Aunt Ellie hug and kiss he loved.

"Are you hungry?"

"No, but I sure would like a Coke," he said, opening the refrigerator.

Marco walked to the coffeemaker and poured a cup.

"Do you want a cup, Ellie?" he asked before setting the pot back.

"Yes. How about we take our drinks out on the terrace?"

Seated comfortably on the overstuffed rattan furniture, Marco casually asked Charles where he and Abigail would be dining after her performance. Ellie, being warned ahead that Charles did not want a big fuss going on or any assuming that he and Abigail were in love, kept her mouth shut, though she was itching to ask a thousand questions.

"Sardi's," Charles answered unenthusiastically, warding off any assumptions his dad or Ellie might have about him "wining and dining" this beautiful woman.

"I love that place," Ellie said.

Marco raised his eyebrows and looked over at her as if to say, *Don't get started.*

"Yah, I made reservations for us, and I'm driving over to Carnegie so I can take her back to her hotel after we eat."

He turned to Ellie and asked what she planned to serve for lunch the next day.

"Your favorite dish, Charlie. Your mom's recipe for chicken á la king over pastry shells. I think a small salad on the side would be nice, and that cake in the kitchen is for dessert."

"Perfect!"

******

At eight the next evening, Charles was sitting in the Carnegie Main Hall, waiting for Abigail to come on stage. He had phoned her late that afternoon to let her know he was in town and told her they would eat at Sardi's after her performance. He had mentioned how anxious his father and Ellie were to see her again. He was totally unaware of how much she prized seeing him again and how wonderful she felt that the weekend had been covered with plans. Much too often, she gave a performance and left the theater alone. Her parents were rarely with her now that she had performances lined up one after another for months to come. Home was more like a pit stop. She was lonely. Applause, loud whistles, and enthusiastic hoots were hardly comparable to the presence of family and the warm touch of a loved one. Tonight, she found herself wanting Charles' company more than anything.

******

Soft lights shadowed over the orchestra while the house lights dimmed. The audience awaited Abigail's entrance onto the stage. As she quickly slipped through the side curtain to step onto stage, the spotlights burst upon her. The audience erupted into clapping and excited cheering. Charles thought his heart would pop out of his chest. In his past imaginations of her, he had forgotten how beautiful she was; or maybe in the past year and a half, she had grown more beautiful.

Her first ballad was a beautiful rendition of "Green Fields," followed by "If He Walked into My Life." Next, a flutist from the orchestra moved to center stage to accompany a lively interpretation of "Never on Sunday." All the ballads were from the sixties and seventies, with melodies in stark contrast from the pop and rock that Broadway was featuring.

A few more songs and some chatting with the audience, Abigail then took a brief intermission and returned wearing a long, shimmering gown, her hair now fixed back from her face in an elegant French twist. It was the last of her program, and she would give her audience just two more songs. The first, "A Time for Us," was sung slowly with expression.

Charles could never deny that he had a lot of Aunt Ellie in his DNA. He was so much like her, it was frightening, but he never wanted to admit it. His thoughts started running in the "Aunt Ellie track" of thinking. He started searching for some intrinsic or spiritual meaning to Abigail singing "A Time for Us." He wanted to find some connection in the lyrics that would point out there was a time for them, and maybe it was now. Willfully, he hung onto one sentence in the song that might refer to them having a life together. He wondered if by some slim chance there was a life for them together.

Next, a guitarist came on stage and joined Abigail. This was the finale—the last gift of the night to her audience. The stage lights were lowered to allow soft spotlights to capture both Abigail and the guitarist. She stood poised while the orchestra played the introduction. At the precise note, the guitar joined in. Charles needed only a moment to identify the song. It was Andrea Bocelli's hit, "Because We Believe," written by David Foster. Chills ran down his spine as Abigail began to sing the English lyrics. So meaningful, the words were meant to encourage dreams and strong beliefs to never give up.

Later at Sardi's, Abigail relaxed with a chilled glass of Perrier. The restaurant was a welcomed setting after working hard to please a packed auditorium of fans. Charles knew the feeling and the exhaustion. He was the perfect person to be with while she came down from the high of a successful performance.

"You were perfect tonight," Charles told her.

"Oh, you're so kind," she said, aiming to be modest.

The food was served, and while they ate and talked, it seemed the evening was getting far into the night.

"I should be getting back to the hotel. It's been a long day," she said, placing her napkin by her plate.

"I know you're tired," he said and immediately called for the check. In no time, they were on their way to the Trump International Hotel and Tower.

"I'll park and walk you in," Charles said, hoping she would know he was simply being thoughtful, not obnoxiously bold.

"Honestly, Charles, you don't need to do that."

He backed off. No need to push it.

"Tomorrow, I'll pick you up at eleven. I'll come into the lobby and have the desk call you."

She was good with that, and he was not the least bit annoyed by simply dropping her off. Tomorrow was the day he was actually looking forward to.

"That's fine," she said as she graciously touched his arm and thanked him for being in the audience and for taking her to dinner.

He took hold of her hand and assured her the pleasure was all his.

"It was great to see you again."

She turned and waved goodbye while walking toward the hotel doors.

******

Pulling out the pins from the French twist, Abigail shook her head to loosen the tight winding. Her hands worked to fluff her hair back into the loose style she preferred. She couldn't believe how tired she felt, yet thrilled to see Charles again. After slipping into a satin nightshirt, she washed her face and brushed her teeth, all the time thinking about him, rather than the usual hashing over of her performance. She called the desk and asked for a wake-up call in the morning.

Turning off the lamp, she whispered a prayer. "Please, God, if it's Your will, let Charles and me start a relationship, but only if he's a Christian."

The paths of love sometimes run on slow avenues, like a year-and-a-half detour. What Charles had yet to discover was that Abigail was a true believer in Christ, and God just might be working behind the scenes to bring them together.

Approaching the A. K. Whittier luxury condominiums and viewing the Gramercy Park area put a wave of nervous butterflies in Abigail's stomach. She had no idea Charles came from a wealthy family. On the flip side, he had no idea she was from a lower middle-class household and that her music education was earned by holding a job while going to school. He knew very little about her.

The sight of the Whittier made her uneasy. She was feeling pressure to play a role—to be something she was not. Her income from performances was going toward paying off her college bills and hopefully give her a place of her own soon. She was sure Charles assumed she was from an affluent family and living in her own apartment or house.

"Well, here we are," Charles said, driving into one of the Ricci parking slots.

"I feel a little nervous," Abigail said while she gathered up her purse and prepared to get out of the car. She felt he might just as well know she was uneasy.

"You shouldn't be one bit nervous. My folks are warm, loving people."

Well, she was there, so what could she do except go through with it?

Riding to the twenty-fifth floor didn't help. Abigail knew from the looks of things all around she was way out of her class.

The elevator doors opened, and directly at hand were Marco and Ellie, standing in the elevator hallway beaming from one ear to the other.

"Your timing is perfect," Marco said, holding his hand out to shake Abigail's. "Ellie just put some shrimp tartlets in the oven."

Abigail entered the penthouse with Ellie's hand softly on her back, sort of happily ushering her inside. Immediately, she was stunned at the beauty of the grand room. Her eyes caught the open entrance to the terrace off to the right and the gallery hallway far in front of her with beautiful paintings hanging on the walls. The evidence of elegance and wealth hit her like a bolt of lightning.

"Oh, this is beautiful," she said.

"Thank you," Marco said, while Ellie motioned for her to set her purse down on the bench in the reception area.

Let's move out onto the terrace," Marco suggested, knowing that the terrace was the best place to relax and break the ice.

And it proved to be the warmth that Charles had assured Abigail would see in his family, for it sparkled like the sun in everything they talked about. Ellie showed her through the penthouse, making mention that her two sons, Anthony and Joe, had once lived there. Abigail loved all of it and especially the large theater room.

"This place is wonderful," she said.

Ellie shook her head in agreement and said, "Let me show you Marco's office. It was my husband's creation." Abigail knew from the conversation on the terrace that Ellie's husband was the architect who grew their business into a billion-dollar success.

She was impressed, and as each moment went by, she found herself realizing their wealth while at the same time relaxing and enjoying their conversations, which were mostly centered on their interest in her career, and Bar Harbor, and wanting to know how much she loved performing in New York City.

Finally, things needed to come to a halt, so Charles suggested they leave and do some touring of the city. He wanted to be alone with her for the time she had left before catching her late flight home.

They ended up in Central Park, watching the pigeons and chatting about all sorts of things, including their family nicknames.

"I noticed your aunt refers to you as Charlie," she said.

"Oh yes, the family calls me Charlie. I was named after Uncle Charles, who went by the name Charley, with a 'y.' What about you? Do you have a family nickname?"

She laughed. "I do. My family calls me Abbie."

"Well, how about we call each other Charlie and Abbie?" he said.

She giggled. "Okay, I like that."

The nicknames were definitely turning their friendship warmer.

This comfortable moment seemed the best time for Abigail to find out if Charles was a believer in Christ like her. The unknown answer had been troubling her ever since she had waved goodbye to him at the Tokyo airport. Seeing him months later and meeting his family made it clear to her that if their friendship was going to move forward, she had to know. It was useless to keep wondering. All she knew was that he was talented and wealthy, and he had good manners. But there was no solid proof that he was a Christian. She wasn't convinced even when his Aunt Ellie referred to their penthouse and architect business being a blessing from God. Nor did Marco's beautiful prayer of thanks that he gave before they ate lunch convince her Charles was of the Christian faith. Before she would go any further in their relationship, she had to know. Finally, she just blurted it out, right there in Central Park, with the first words that came to her mind.

"Charlie, you need to know that I'm a Christian and Jesus is the center of my life."

She stopped walking and looked at him, waiting for his reaction.

******

Wow! Her statement came at him like a football tossed directly over the heads of all the players and landing in his hands. Charles' heart felt like it skipped more than a couple beats. A third missed beat and his legs would have buckled him to the ground. He was as anxious as her to know if they shared each other's faith. Now with the ball landing solidly in his hands, he pulled it in and quickly ran for the touchdown.

"Abbie," he said, taking her hand, "the Lord is the center of my life, too. Without Him, I'm lost and can do nothing. This is fantastic! We are on the same ground. Believe me, I wanted to know where you stood with God, but I couldn't find the right time or the words to ask. I'm so glad you told me."

He gathered her into his arms—right there in Central Park with people and pigeons all around them—and kissed her.

Then, as though the sun had popped out from behind a cloud, he said, "How about we get some ice cream? There's an ice cream parlor around the corner on Fifth Avenue."

That was a perfect idea, bound to keep the conversation flowing. Eat ice cream and walk down Fifth Avenue. What could be better?

Slowly strolling down Fifth Avenue with the fun of enjoying double dips of mint chocolate chip and butter pecan ice cream cones, Charles came up with a brilliant thought to keep Abigail with him.

"Hey, I've got a great idea," he said. "How about we spend the rest of your time today back at the penthouse? Aunt Ellie loves to have company for dinner."

"Are you sure?" she asked.

"Of course!"

"Okay, but make sure I get back to the hotel in time to pick up my things and get to the airport."

Instead of Ellie fixing dinner or sending out, they went to La Grenouille, a French restaurant located in Midtown.

"You'll love their buttery Dover sole fish," Marco said, knowing the restaurant's menu like the back of his hand and being one of their prime customers.

They hailed a cab, and all four of them squeezed in tight and headed to the restaurant.

It was late when Charles brought Abigail back to the hotel.

"I'll wait here in the lobby," he told her, hardly getting the words out before she darted off to the elevators. In a jiffy, she was back with her suitcase in hand and a large purse hanging off her shoulder. She was wearing a sweatshirt and black jeans, looking like a teenager, rather than a sophisticated soprano who had performed at Carnegie Hall just a day ago.

"It's colder at Bar Harbor than here," she said, excusing her attire.

"You look fantastic to me," Charles said.

They walked outside and stood near the curb. Charles was in no hurry to hail a cab. He wanted a few moments to tell her how much he enjoyed being with her.

He set her suitcase on the ground and looked at her.

"I hate to see you go, Abbie," he said.

"Me, too, Charlie," she said, allowing him to get closer.

He leaned in, pulling her close to him as their lips melted together.

Keeping his arms around her, he kissed her again.

She let go and got into the cab. But before the cab door closed, he leaned in and said, "I'll call you tomorrow."

Chapter 4

Charles was considering flying to Bar Harbor to visit Abigail, but coming to the house she lived in was a dreadful matter for her to accept after seeing the penthouse he was brought up in and all the luxuries his family owned. It was like oil trying to mix with water. It wouldn't work. She was embarrassed and ashamed of her common roots and desired to keep the relationship right where it was, which was ridiculous because she wanted more than just a friendly relationship with him.

On the same token, how would he react when he saw her humble house and considered the environment in which she was raised? Indeed, her background was miles apart from his, but it wasn't just the difference in their background that troubled her, but the reaction of her parents when they learned she was in love with Charles Ricci, the wealthy pianist. Her father would be uncompromising.

She tried every excuse in the book to keep Charles from visiting her. She wanted time to work things out. Maybe if she could string him along until she got enough money to have her own luxury place, then she could allow him to visit. Such nonsense! Abigail knew he would never stay away.

Their phone conversation was thorny and problematic when visiting was brought up. Finally, she leveled with him.

"Charlie, I'm not sure how you will feel about my parents—or me—when you see how ordinary we live. We're not rich. You need to know that I come from a blue-collar family. I grew up in an entirely different environment than you."

She waited for him to respond.

When he did, he expressed shock that she felt threatened by his wealth. What did that have to do with being in love? He didn't care if they lived in a shack or if she had no education and no money. All the outside stuff meant nothing. He loved her for who she was and what was inside her heart.

"Abbie, what do you take me for? I'm not in love with you because I think your father is king of Mount Desert Island there in Bar Harbor."

That was a real zinger he threw! He must have Googled Bar Harbor and saw that island on the map.

He waited for her to respond; but she held back, and then he heard her crying. She was unprepared to hear him say that he truly loved her, though she felt the same toward him. But beyond their common ground of music and their careers in the entertainment world, if she discovered that the difference in their heritage posed a problem, she wanted no part of getting serious with him. It would be too hurtful. There was a lot to work through if they were going to allow their feelings for one another to develop—mainly, her career because she was reaching close to the top and her parents were dead set that she keep pushing to reach her goal. Her father would not want her involved with the Ricci family, nor any family, if it would interfere with her career. She could hear him yelling right now, "They're uppity, rich people; you don't belong with them."

He was dead wrong if he said that. She knew they were not uppity people. Rich, yes, but far from being haughty.

But the truth remained that she was way different in background, and no matter how successful and famous she might become and how involved with Charles she might get, her common heritage would always be part of her.

"Oh, Charlie, I didn't plan on this, but I have fallen in love with you, too.

She sniffled back her tears and went on.

"My father will be furious if he thinks you will interfere with my career. I don't know about you coming here. Maybe you should wait."

"Wait for what? We're in love!" he bellowed into the phone. "Your father has his place, but he's not the authority over your life. I don't think for one minute that it was a coincidence that you were booked to share the stage with me in Tokyo. Remember how we talked in the park just a week ago? We acknowledged that it was something other than fate that put us together. We share our common faith in Jesus Christ. I believe God had all this planned. I felt something the moment I saw you. I went home and tried to push it out of my mind, but I could not stop what was going on in my heart. You see what happened. We met again, and we fell in love."

While he kept trying to convince her, she remembered many conversations with her mother when things were not working out or seemed difficult. She could hear her saying, "Abigail, everything works out for the best if you are trusting the Lord."

There was no use fighting it. If Charles was right for her, it would work out.

"Well, then, when would you want to come?" she questioned.

"I was thinking this weekend. I'll get a room at a hotel and rent a car and let you plan the rest."

"All right. I'll work things out on my end, but it's not going to be easy. You don't know my father."

There was a definite crossroad stretched out in front of her. She had time to choose either way. If she refused Charles, it might mean the loss of a life filled with love and happiness. She might let go of a world and a life she would never find again. Could she take the risk of following her emotions rather than her career and still end up singing for the world? With Charles pulling on one end and her father pulling on the other, how could she come to the right decision? If she could not please them both, maybe she should be true to herself. The truth was that her father was not a happy man to begin with. He was like a tyrant when it came to getting his way. No one pushed Rod Clark, not even his daughter. He was a strongminded, willful man. Abigail's faith and refinement were the result of her mother's influence. Irene Clark was the reason her daughter had gained scholarships and made it through her studies and auditions to become a rising star. Tension was always high in the house because of the division between her father's agnostic attitude and her mother's faith. Charles had no idea what he was up against.

It was best that she confide only in her mother about being in love with Charles. His visit would have to be cast as something other than telling her father they were in love. Besides, they had no marriage plans. This was just the beginning. She might back out if she thought it was too difficult.

******

Irene liked Charles right from the start, so she had no problem with her daughter getting into a relationship with him. That night in Tokyo, sitting in the audience and hearing how beautifully he played each medley, she was greatly touched. The expressions on his face as he brought his soul into each selection he played were captivating, and she found herself in a world of beautiful harmony and God-inspired talent. His music seemed to demonstrate how wonderful Heaven might be. She would do all she could to help make Charles' visit pleasant.

In the meantime, Charles was perfectly honest with his family about what he was planning to do. He let them know he was in love with Abigail soon after she left New York, the weekend of her performance at Carnegie Hall.

"I don't know where this is leading, I just know that I love her and want to be with her every minute I can," he told his father. He let Ellie in on it, too.

His family sensed his tension in getting to know Abigail's parents and having them approve of him.

"She wasn't born with a silver spoon in her mouth," he told them. "Her background is low totem pole. She's had to work for everything she has. Her mother is her biggest support. Her father is a tyrant— at least from what she told me, I would classify him as an oppressing dictator. I don't know if I can work this out with him."

"Wow, Charlie, that's pretty harsh," Marco said. But he remembered how he had felt when he considered how much he loved Charles' mother, Katie, and the difficulty they had had at first.

******

Marco would never forget his own struggle and Katie's refusal to go to New York with him and spend Christmas with Ellie and her husband, Charley. As a result of her refusal, he purposely chose Christmas Eve to leave Fairview, as if to hurt their situation further. Walking up that snowy hill with a suitcase in hand, he stood at the top overlooking the village of Fairview, painfully letting go of the last bit of his life with her. It seemed fitting to let his unhappiness infest his soul.

Through the falling snow, he saw the lights of the church twinkling below, as though they were winking at him and saying, Don't leave. *He could hear the words of "Silent Night" streaming out of the church, circling the hill, the words almost hypercritical. No one was standing there with him, but he heard it again—that inner voice, the waned summons telling him he must go. Its message seemed crystal clear, bidding him to depart the hilly countryside of Fairview and embark upon another life. Things were too difficult to keep pursuing her.*

During those moments long ago, there seemed to be no hint of anything good happening that might allow something safe and wholesome to come to pass. His spirit was dead under the concrete truth that she was not free. His life lay at his feet as though it were ashes rather than roses. She belonged to another man, a man lying in a care facility on a motorized bed with oxygen pumping continuously. Her husband was like a dead man to Katie, all because of his carnal temper that drove him off on a motorcycle after an argument. In his madness, he had crashed into a ravine.

This was a completely different situation than Charles' problem with Abigail, but the reality of the circumstances meant that unless God intervened, they would never be together.

There was a deeply hidden secret that Charles would never know. Katie was not his real mother. All Charles knew of his bloodline was his father's family and what little bit there was to Katie's family, which spoke only of distant cousins she had lost track of and a deceased uncle. He saw only pictures of Katie's deceased parents, nothing more. The unknown lay safe in infinity, and to Marco and Ellie, it would stay there. Charles was Marco's son, and he was rescued from evil. And that settled it. The dark secret of his real mother having a one-night stand with his father was a forgiven sin. The woman died of a deliberate overdose of drugs after he was born. Charles need never be told. As for God's opinion in this situation—Katie, Marco, and Ellie had peace that the Lord was okay with this hushed secret. They had peace because Charles came to Katie as a newborn and knew only her as his mother. Subconsciously, the family treated him with extra care and attention, all because of the deeply hidden secret. Their attention came naturally, as automatic responsiveness without deliberate thought.

Marco had repented of his adultery and was honest to tell Katie about his mistake before he married her. She loved him enough to forgive this mistake. It was after they were married that the baby was born. And just a few days later, the woman swallowed an overdose of drugs and died. Charles need never know. What good would it do to tell him this story? God's forgiveness and the love he shared with Katie and his father need never be tarnished by this woman's evil behavior and his father's forgiven mistake. Katie and Marco had nurtured Charles into a wonderful, Christian man.

Bringing his focus back to the subject of Charles and Abigail, Marco seriously looked at Charles and said, "Charles, please take it slow and don't make any rash judgments. If this is right for you and Abigail, it will eventually work out."

"I want to believe that, Dad, but Abbie was crying when she told me about her situation. It's got to be bad."

Ellie put her arms around him and just held tight for a moment. There wasn't a lot left to be said. They simply needed to believe that if it was meant for him to be with Abigail, God would make a way.

******

Charles was performing just one concert in Denver before flying to Bar Harbor. It was an afternoon performance at the prestigious Arts Complex, located in the heart of the theater district. He would fly home right after the last song and leave the next morning on an early, non-stop flight to Bangor, Maine, the closest airport to Bar Harbor.

With the short time left at home before leaving for Denver the next day, he went through the monotonous practice of playing major and minor scales and then all his selections for the concert.

Sarah noticed that he was struggling a little at the keyboard and knew it was undoubtedly caused by his thoughts for that woman she had heard him discussing with Natalie. Her awareness of this woman was that she was simply a soprano named Abigail Clark. She knew that he was going to Bar Harbor to be with her, though he never mentioned he was in love with her. But Sarah made a good guess about the situation. No doubt she'd be hearing more and more of this woman. There was a twinge of motherly jealousy poking at her. She was the one caring for him and his house and domestically involved in much of his life. She didn't want any intrusions. In her jealous thoughts, she imagined that this woman might move in on what she claimed was her territory.

******

Charles' struggle to concentrate at the keyboard would end once he was on stage tomorrow, but in the relaxed atmosphere of the music room, he had a hard time pushing distracting thoughts away. He began working on the pop song he planned to perform at the end of his concert. The practice of playing and singing a pop song was becoming a regular occurrence. It was now a performance signature. Every audience was expecting this at the end of his program. For Denver, he chose the 1965 rendition of "The Shadow of Your Smile." Those haunting words generated feelings for Abbie. *The shadow of your smile when you are gone, Will color all my dreams...*[3]

Sarah stepped into the room and startled his thoughts.

"Would you like dinner in the dining room?"

"No, just bring it to my office, please. I've got some paperwork to tend to this evening that cannot wait."

"I hope you don't mind me being so bold, sir, but it doesn't seem as though you've been resting well."

"I'm sure I'll be okay, and I'll rest well tonight. Thank you, Sarah."

Denver was a sold-out audience, and they loved the excitement of hearing him play and sing a ballad. Charles brought the floor mic to the piano and sang the lyrics as though he was announcing to Denver that he was in love. The next morning, he boarded a plane again, this time flying northeast and arriving at the Bangor International

---

3   Jack Sheldon, "The Shadow of Your Smile," *The Sandpiper*, No. 1, Verve Music, 1965.

Airport early in the morning. From there, he drove forty-five miles in a rented car to Abbie's house.

He found her street without driving into the heart of town or seeing the harbor. Turning the car down the road she lived on, he noticed the neighborhood was lined with cookie-cutter bungalows. The trees were huge, having been planted decades ago, probably right after World War Two. Most of the houses were well cared for, and he knew to keep driving toward the end of the block and look for the address number on the curb mailbox. The area was a far cry from his place in Connecticut. The harbor area was several yards away and blocked by trees and green brush. He could not get a good view of it from the street.

Abigail was peering out the front window when he drove into the driveway. The sight of her brought a rush of emotion. Perhaps she had forgotten how much she loved him, and now the spark of affection was being ignited again, much like how she felt in New York City. She opened the door and embraced him as though she wanted to melt in his arms, forgetting they were supposed to be just friends.

"Did you have any trouble finding us?" she questioned.

"No, your directions from the airport were perfect, but I had the GPS running, too," he said, pulling away from her to not appear like he wanted to kiss her.

"Come on in," she said, opening the door wide.

The place was pleasant. Nice furniture, colorful themes throughout, and a remodeled kitchen that showed off beautiful granite counters. It was a modest place that reflected good taste that was attractively done; but any project in this small, seven-room, story-and-a-half bungalow had to be a challenge.

Rod was decent to him. He shook his hand. Obviously conditioned that the visit was a friendly social call from this so-called entertainer he had met in Tokyo. In contrast, Irene was a perfect hostess, offering beverages and conversation and tending to the dinner she would serve later that afternoon.

Abigail seemed shy, which made Charles a little uneasy because he hoped she was not acting that way due to embarrassment. The scene was uncomfortable, if not a bit on the weird side. Her dad was not talkative, which didn't help. Irene and Abigail carried the brunt of the conversation. The only thing that seemed to save some of the awkwardness was Abigail's spunky black-and-white shih tzu named Molly, who took to Charles like a family member.

Irene was an excellent cook, and Charles found that she was better at it than his Aunt Ellie's chef, who cooked for all their holiday gatherings and special occasions, and even better than Sarah.

Although no one knew what Charles liked most to eat, Irene knew he wasn't a vegetarian, and that meant he was a man who loved meat and potatoes. Her menu was prime rib roast with all the trimmings, along with an elegant dessert of what she guessed might be one of his favorites, New York cheesecake with raspberry sauce.

She made a hit with Charles!

The conversation around the dinner table moved into a warm, cordial milieu. Funny how food can make everything seem better. Even Molly, who was keeping an eye on Charles and occasionally begging, brought the atmosphere to a comfortable level that he appreciated, even beyond his proper manners that would never allow a dog to beg at the table. Proper table manners were drilled into him from the moment he grew out of the highchair. No talking with your mouth full; no pushing bread in the gravy with your fingers; no licking your knife; and definitely no burping out loud. But here at this modest home, Charles was so relaxed, he went for second helpings after Rod helped himself.

******

Abigail sat across the table from him, and every now and then, when her father was busy shoveling food in his mouth, he winked at her. She wanted to snicker and laugh out loud because she knew what those sweet winks meant—*I love this food; I love your mom; I love you;* and *I'll get your dad eating out of my hand.* Oh, how she loved him! It seemed to her that God was putting His blessing on their relationship right there at the table, and the bumps would get worked out.

After dinner, Abigail wanted to show Charles all of Bar Harbor, and show it she did! He constantly commented on how amazing everything was—the stunning coastal beauty and the many yachts and lobster boats anchored offshore. The view of small islands in the distance and the ocean connecting all of it displayed a setting that could range from glistening sunlight to misty fog. He was awestruck at the many gorgeous homes and mansions peppered along the shoreline. He realized that Bar Harbor was a distinctive waterfront city, filled with beauty, wealth, and common people.

"Abbie, this place is beautiful," he said to her as they walked the popular shoreline.

"I love it here," she told him. "Many of the residents are retired or just plain underemployed and making a lifestyle choice."

"I can see why," Charles said.

******

Charles was thinking that Bar Harbor could be a place for them to have a vacation home. Only a six-hour drive from Greenwich, which would make it a perfect getaway. They could leave Connecticut at six in the morning and be in Bar Harbor by noon. Or they could fly if they didn't feel like driving. He kept that thought to himself, not wanting to rush things. First thing he needed to deal with was getting Rod Clark's blessing to marry Abbie.

He left that evening reluctant to say too much before parting for his hotel. The early flight the next morning out of Bangor meant he would not see Abigail the next day. He sensed that Rod knew his daughter was in love with him. He hoped after he was gone there would not be an ugly family dispute.

She walked out to the car with him. It was useless to hide their feelings. They embraced and kissed.

"I love you and your house and all about Bar Harbor," he told her. "I've never felt so much at home with someone as I have here, including your parents."

"Even my dad?" she questioned, laughing.

"I don't think he's going to be hard to win over," he said, feeling confident.

"I hope you're right. I just hope I don't walk into a hornet's nest when I go back into the house."

"Just stay calm if there's trouble. You've done nothing wrong, except fall in love with me," he said with a slight chuckle.

"Call me when you get back to Greenwich tomorrow, okay?"

"I will," he said. "I'll miss you."

He kissed her again and opened the car door and then turned to her.

"When you sing at the Majestic Theater in New York three weeks from now, let's cook up something to get your parents to accompany you, and we'll plan a dinner party at the penthouse."

"Oh, Charlie, I don't know if my dad would go for that," she said, sounding like it would be easier to get Spain and Britain to agree to share ownership of the Rock of Gibraltar.

"We've got three weeks to work on it. Leave it to me—and my dad and Aunt Ellie. We will get your parents to the penthouse and wanting to come back."

He started the car and put the window down.

"You know I love you," he said as he started a slow roll backward down the driveway. "I'll call you as soon as I get home tomorrow."

Charles turned over every stone, flipped on every switch, played every angle, and prayed harder than ever before; and it paid off. Rod and Irene were accompanying Abigail to New York City for her performance at the Majestic Theater, and they accepted the invitation to the penthouse for a late dinner party afterward. This was the first miracle Charles needed in order to marry Abbie with her parent's blessing, and it assured him that God was directing things.

Ellie called the maid in to help but instructed her to leave before everyone came back from the theater. Having the chef in the kitchen and the maid serving dinner was clearly out of order for this dinner party. If Ellie could pull this off well, she would have Irene and

Abigail helping her get the food on the table and cleaning things up after dinner. And while they were doing that, Marco and Charles would be out on the terrace with Rod, engaging him in conversation that would prove they were truly interested in him and not uppity snobs that looked down on people from different walks of life.

Everything was working like a charm. Abigail's performance was spectacular, which was no surprise to anyone. She sang like an angel, and the audience loved her.

Back at the penthouse afterward, things were going as planned.

"What do you do in Bar Harbor?" Marco asked Rod. That question started a lengthy oration of his job as a captain of a lobster boat. Of course, the boat was owned by someone else, but Rod ran it and was paid a regular salary.

"So, how is this done?" Marco asked. "What are the restrictions that the government puts on fishing?" He was truly captivated at this line of work.

Rod went into great detail, and Charles was amazed at how interesting lobster fishing was. Actually, both he and Marco were quite impressed.

"I'd love to see that in action," Marco said. "Any chance I could come and go for a run with you?"

Charles immediately spoke up. "I'd like to do that, too!"

"Oh, sure," Rod said. "I can take both of you out on a run any time you like."

Marco and Charles looked at each other like they had just won the grand prize for Abigail.

"Great," Marco responded. "We'll look at our calendars and give you a call to set something up."

The rest of the evening was spent talking about everything from politics to cars and looking at photos of some of Marco's architect projects when the men gathered in his office.

Ellie easily pulled Irene and Abigail into the chore of helping to clear the table and get the dishes rinsed and in the dishwasher. This was her strategy of assuring them that she was like any other housewife. The chef and the maid could be introduced to them some other time. As soon as the kitchen was back in order, she took Irene into every room, with Abigail following, and explained the many designs her husband, Charley, created, pointing out some of his handy architect talent that made the penthouse extraordinary. She talked about her grown sons, Anthony and Joe, hoping that someday Irene and Rod would meet them, explaining that they lived in New York City and worked with Marco. Everything she mentioned and did was in an effort to make Abigail and her parents feel at home and to know that they had much common ground.

Only with casual reference was anything said about Charles and Abigail's relationship. When the time was right, Charles would ask for Rod and Irene's blessing to marry Abigail. When and how it would be done, he didn't know. But first, he had to propose to her.

It didn't take long to discover what the reality was between the Clarks and the Riccis. In every walk of life and every financial level, there is always common ground to meet on if it is searched for. They seemed to be finding it.

Marco and Charles loved the lobster run and did it again. They were like kids learning to fish. A true friendship was building amongst the three of them. Before long, Rod was invited to tour the

Ricci architect headquarters and fly with Marco on the company jet to one of his projects, which he accepted at Abigail's amazement. She could not understand what made her dad mellow down and act decent, except that Marco's interest in the lobster business and not knowing one thing about it made her dad feel important. All the anxiety and apprehension she had suffered earlier about him accepting Charles was unnecessary. Things were moving along well, and there was no other way to explain it but that God was in it.

Weeks were passing, and Abigail had not yet been invited to Greenwich. Charles was saving the shoreline of Long Island Sound for the setting he would propose marriage to her. It was tough waiting for a weekend when neither of them was performing, but finally, it came. He booked a flight for her and made sure that both families knew Sarah would be there, so everything would be proper. Of course, Sarah, being old enough to be their grandmother and feeling like a godparent to Charles, would chaperone them well.

He was as nervous as a tightrope walker when he picked her up at the airport and brought her to his place.

******

Stepping onto the cobblestone walkway in front of Charles' home, Abigail was charmed. The soft sound of waves on the beach caught her attention, and she turned to look.

"That's Long Island Sound you're looking at," he told her.

"Oh, it's beautiful," she said.

Walking the long pathway toward the entrance, she remarked about the pear trees—how stunningly they flanked both sides of the walkway making the path seem like a trail. A nervous excitement came over her as she realized she was about to enter the beautiful stone and brick mansion of the man she loved, the man she hoped to marry.

Stepping inside, her amazement continued as she scanned the relaxed décor that felt warm, yet elegant and radiating with class.

Sarah met them in the entrance hall.

"Sarah, this is Abigail Clark," he said.

Abbie held out her hand and said, "Hello, please call me Abbie."

"Hello," Sarah said cheerfully.

Charles took her suitcase to the bedroom and gave the room a quick glance, noticing that Sarah had fixed it up for a queen. There were fresh flowers on the dresser and small dishes of imported chocolates on the table near the plush wingback chair. The bathroom counter had several molded soaps and special jars of fragrant creams. A new terrycloth robe was placed over the small, upholstered bench near the large, claw-footed tub.

"Oh, that wonderful Sarah," said Charles. "She thinks of everything."

As soon as Abigail freshened up, Charles showed her the garden terrace and the blue Caribbean indoor pool.

"Charlie, your home is magnificent! I can't imagine how wonderful it must be to live here."

"Thank you," he happily responded. "I'm quite comfortable here. All of this is from my imagination and vivid images of how I wanted the place to look. My father did some fantastic architect management, too." He led her back into the great room and up to the bar area and offered her something to drink.

"I really do love it here," he said, while stepping behind the bar. "But it does actually get a bit lonely at times when I'm not busy with my music."

"I can imagine," she responded, remembering that he often called her two and three times a day.

"What can I get you to drink, darling," he asked.

"I'd love to have a Perrier water."

He poured the same for himself, and then offered a toast.

"Here's to us and a happy future," he said, clicking his glass to hers and taking a big gulp. Both of them burst into laughter. Charles leaned in close and kissed her.

Dinner was served in the terrace garden, where a fuel firepit was lit and keeping the air warm. As soon as Sarah tidied up the kitchen and went to her quarters, Charles and Abigail changed into comfortable jogging sweats and went for a walk on the beach. Charles' plan was to propose to her in the moonlight.

Walking along the sandy beach, he stopped for a moment and said, "Look at that moon. Isn't it huge and bright? Makes you feel you could reach out and touch it."

He fumbled around in his pocket while she was looking at the moon and brought the ring out.

Kneeling on one knee, he took her hand and said, "Abbie, I love you and want you to be my wife. Will you marry me?"

Her hands went up to her face in surprise. She had no idea he was going to propose marriage on the beach and do it just hours after arriving at his home.

"Oh yes, I will marry you, Charlie," she said, holding back tears and throwing her arms around him. Then putting her hand out, he slipped the ring on her finger.

He brought her close into him and gently caressed her face and brushed her hair back and kissed her.

The waves were washing calmly ashore in a steady rhythm that seemed like the heartbeat of a thousand angels. Charles was handsome in the moonlight. His face tan and his hair slightly bleached from the summer sun. He looked so much like his Sicilian father. She wondered, *How can I be so fortunate to find a man like this? I am nothing compared to him, yet he is loving me and wanting me. I feel like I'm Cinderella, and my foot fits the glass slipper. I want to live forever right here.*

They walked slowly back to the house, hand in hand, and he said to her, "When you go back home, Abbie, I want to go with you and ask your parents for their blessing."

Chapter 5

The few days Abigail spent at the Greenwich mansion sailed by quickly. She was comfortable there and wished she could stay forever. Early morning swims in the pool, lunches in the terrace garden, and walks on the beach were like stepping into another world. Charles kept hoping that after they were married, she would make the Greenwich mansion her own. Certainly, he would understand if she wanted to start fresh at another place, but he loved this magnificent house and hoped she would agree to make it their permanent home.

Greenwich was a wealthy city. It was not a place Abigail would choose on her own, but with Charles, it was starting to feel like home. Everything was captivating—the walks through the historic center, window shopping on Greenwich Avenue, happy tourists taking pictures, and people eating at the sidewalk cafes.

One evening, she and Charles enjoyed a romantic dinner at the Blue Hill Stone Barn. They ordered fresh-caught seafood and ate on the veranda. Another evening, Charles drove her through the most prestigious section of the city to show off the wealth of Greenwich and the New England-style mansions. Nothing compared to what he owned, but if she wanted a fresh start, there were options open for her to choose.

The train station, oddly enough, held the most interest for her when she learned they could visit Marco and Ellie in New York City by taking a fifty-minute train ride rather than driving. Truly, without saying much in favor of keeping Charles' mansion, the whisper of acceptance was there in her smiles. The tipoff seemed to be the train and the beach at Long Island Sound.

The last evening before traveling back to Bar Harbor, Charles sat at the grand piano and invited Abigail to sit with him on the bench. He played several songs for her, and she hummed along, even breaking into singing a few times. And then, impromptu, he stopped playing and said, "This is the song that sums up how I feel about you." He played a song from the musical, *The Music Man*—"Till There Was You." Abigail blushed as he sang the words.

The words were romantic and appropriate, as though the song was written just for him to tell the story of how bland his life was until he met her. He became the one in the song who never knew there were bells on the hill, or roses, or fragrant meadows, or love all around until she came into his life.

Back in Bar Harbor, Abigail was welcomed by her mother as though she had been gone for months. Then quickly, her mother turned her attention to Charles and gave him a hug, as though she had missed him, too. Her father was his usual self, sitting in his recliner forgetting that good manners meant he should get up and say hello.

"How was your trip?" her mother asked, knowing they had passed through heavy rain from Bangor all the way to Bar Harbor.

"Not bad," Charles said, taking off his jacket and helping Abigail with her coat.

From that point on, their arrival turned into an ordinary visit until Charles took the opportunity to let them know he had asked their daughter to marry him, adding that she had said yes to his proposal.

Her dad quickly released the footrest of the recliner and sat straight up. In an insensitive, rude manner, he said, "You better think hard about this, Abigail. You'll ruin your career if you get married."

An icy atmosphere filled the room.

Her mom tried to take the chill off by making an attempt to calm her husband down.

"Now, Rod, let's give them a chance to talk to us."

Abigail's emotions started building quickly. *Here it is,* she thought to herself. *It never fails. He's the killjoy. His finger is always on the trigger.* But she held her peace while Charles spoke softly.

"I love your daughter, and she loves me. We both have careers and understand that we will often be performing away from each other. That goes with the territory of being entertainers. But we do not consider this to be a problem. We have talked things over and cannot find any reason that would hint that we cannot have a wonderful life together. You can be assured that I would never allow anything to happen that would harm our marriage. I love Abigail, and I will take care of her. She's made the choice to marry me, and I was hoping that we could have your blessing."

Then Abigail spoke up, her lips trembling as she worked to keep control of her emotions.

"I hope you will not expect me to make a choice between Charles and you, because my choice is Charles."

Her mother looked over at her father as if to say, "It's been settled, so you better get on board, or we will lose our daughter."

It was a powerful moment. A life-changing moment, no matter which way it went. The outcome could be a wonderful beginning for all of them, if her father realized that his daughter was not under his exclusive authority and that her allegiance was not to him or her mother. The other outcome would separate Abigail from her parents if her dad selfishly played the spoilsport and refused his blessing.

Her father got up out of the recliner and walked toward Charles, as though he had just lost a fierce battle. Holding his hand out, he said, "You win, Charlie boy. I won't stand in your way; and as long as you love her and promise to take proper care of her, you have my blessing."

Charles stood up and shook his hand, although he did not like being called Charlie boy. It was an insult and probably not the last from him.

"Thank you, sir. You have my word."

The rest of the visit went well. Abigail showed her ring and briefly discussed tentative wedding plans. She wanted the wedding ceremony to be at their church in Bar Harbor.

******

The cold, strained air in the small bungalow went to warm and manageable, as soon as the important matter of Charles and Abigail's engagement was resolved. Charles insisted they celebrate by going out for dinner. He suggested the Sea Captain Restaurant that overlooked a long stretch of the harbor and gave a view of the islands in the distance. His decision suited all of them, so off they went, Charles feeling relieved.

The floor-to-ceiling windows of the restaurant stretched around three sides of the dining area, giving them a panoramic view of offshore sailboats, some of them clustered in small groups and docked tightly together in the water. A cruise ship surprisingly passed through the harbor while they were eating. No one had a clue that Charles had found this restaurant on the internet back in Greenwich, when he struggled about how he might handle things with Abigail's parents. In his opinion, this restaurant was the perfect place—not too highfalutin but nice enough to be comfortable. His presumption paid off. The nervous atmosphere between them began to melt away.

In the few hours left before Charles planned to depart for the airport at Bangor, many more things were talked about and agreed upon concerning the wedding. Soon, however, he was well washed-out with the stress of this visit and wanted to get on his way. But Irene insisted he stay and leave early the next morning. There was no room for escape, not with Abigail also begging him to stay. Charles was outnumbered.

He ended up sleeping in the small guest bedroom upstairs. It felt strange and out of the ordinary to be bedding down there, in a tiny bedroom that was almost suffocating. He was definitely in a world he'd never experienced before. This house and this bedroom were nothing like the luxury of the penthouse and the bedroom he slept in before he left home. That spacious bedroom was originally designed for his cousin Anthony but became his when Anthony moved out. If the Clarks slept in that bedroom, they would think they had stepped onto another planet. There was no comparison of this tiny upstairs bedroom to what he was accustomed to, and it felt strange. He hoped morning would come quickly so he could graciously leave and be on his way.

He laid across the bed, imagining the bedroom he grew up in, as though he could jump into it and escape this common, little place. He could see his old bedroom as plain as day, reflecting Ellie's awesome decorating talent. The room showcased a wide, thick-cushioned headboard that stretched sixteen-feet high from the floor to the ceiling. The massive headrail produced a breathtaking focus toward the king-size bed that rested on top of a tufted, black leather, upholstered platform. A giant sunburst mirror hung artistically on the textured, avocado green wall across from the bed. To the left of the bed, a credenza accommodated a large, propped-up painting of something so weird, it could claim a title from anyone's imagination. The Italian marble floor was accented by two expansive Oriental rugs. Scattered throughout the room were silver lamps topped with black shades. A manly-sized lounging chair often held his clothes when he was too lazy to hang them up.

The room went on and on to the farthest corner, where an archway led into a walk-in closet, so spacious it could be turned into a dance floor. Rows of shelves and columns of drawers lined the walls, running from floor to ceiling. Shiny, varnished wood hangers dangled on silver-toned clothes rods. A large, black leather ottoman sat on white, luxurious carpet in the center of the closet. The penthouse bedroom was a far cry from this upstairs room that held only a bed, small dresser, and a wooden chair without arms.

But nonetheless, there was something warm and cozy about this room. Something about the entire house that mysteriously charmed him. Everything about this house and about Abigail being brought up here made him feel that his life in New York City may have missed a lot. He actually envied her for how she lived and worked to get everything she had. In his judgment, she deserved the stardom she was receiving. She earned it well, and her parents could be proud of her.

As for Rod, he respected him after taking two runs with him on the lobster boat. He truly was a hardworking man, in spite of being harsh and unreasonable at times. The proof of his hard work was in this modest bungalow that embarrassed Abigail. The evidence of his hard labor was everywhere in this house—from the delicious food on their table, and the nice clothes on their backs, and all the necessities that kept them comfortable. Rod faithfully provided for his family, and Charles was giving him credit. As for Irene, he put her in the same wonderful category as Aunt Ellie.

Glancing through the wooden blinds that didn't quite reach the sill of the narrow upper window, he stared at the cookie-cutter bungalows across the street, shadowed by the gas streetlights that dotted the neighborhood. He felt the vast culture distance between him and the people living in those common houses, and it seemed that he would gain something good by being accepted by Abbie's parents. It was becoming real to him that the burden of acceptance was not so much on them, but on him. He needed to work on gracefully enduring the Clarks with humbleness, and they, in turn, were meekly welcoming him into their family. As for his point of view of Abigail, she was learning that love could conquer humiliation. Looking at things from all angles, he wasn't sure if he should be thankful about being rich and having material luxuries or thankful that he was witnessing a different kind of human contentment to which he had never been exposed.

Slipping out of his clothes, he snuggled down under the cotton sheets and the homemade quilt and fell asleep.

******

Both families were buzzing with wedding plans, and Abigail made it plain to her mother, and to Ellie as well, that she did not want a reception of epic proportions. But things got out of her control when Charles insisted that she choose a designer wedding gown. She could not insult him and refuse his generous offer to charge the gown to his account. So, she went to New York City with her mother, retrieved Ellie from the penthouse, and the three of them went to the LaFabre Bridal Salon, where she selected an Oscar de la Renta design. The gown was breathtaking. Flowing gracefully from her waist to the floor with delicate Chantilly lace laid over lustrous charmeuse satin. Irene was so overtaken with the beauty of her daughter walking out of the dressing room in that gown, tears trickled down her cheeks.

"You look absolutely stunning in that gown, sweetheart," she said, wiping the tears from her cheeks.

"Oh, Mom, I love this gown. I don't think I need to try another one on," she said glancing over at Ellie for her approval.

"I agree with both of you," Ellie chimed in while nodding her head. "This gown looks like it was make for you."

For the two bridesmaids—her best friends from her college years—she chose autumn colors of deep plum to accommodate the October wedding.

They decided on England as their honeymoon destination. An early afternoon wedding ceremony with dinner served immediately was planned so they could go back to Greenwich and leave for England the next morning.

Everything was in whirlwind mode. Irene was superb in helping them choose the right place for the reception, which ended up at the elegant, oceanside Bar Harbor Regency Resort. The guest list was an intimate size of fifty people. Guest rooms were reserved and paid for by the Ricci family, and reservations for the championship golf course were offered for those who wished to play golf the next day. It was turning out to be a wedding of epic proportions, regardless of Abigail's wishes.

The dining area was as plush as the New York penthouse. Place settings were a royal design of blue and gold edging. White, floor-length tablecloths and full-length chair covers gave the dining area an authentic wedding look. Charles and Abigail chose a combination Sicilian and European menu.

A small orchestra assembled at the back of the dance floor after toasts were carried out by Anthony and Joe, who took advantage of pleasantly roasting their cousin, Charles, and then ending with a warm and loving speech welcoming Abigail to the Ricci family.

Almost unbelievably, Rod got up and toasted his daughter and new son-in-law with a loving and accepting speech, which brought some tears to Abigail. The entire event was the best anyone could have hoped for.

As soon as the bridal dance was over and Abigail had danced with her father and Marco, the bride and groom hurried to change clothes and scoot off to the parking lot, where Anthony was waiting to drive them to the Bangor airport.

Charles couldn't wait to pull Abbie close to him while they snuggled in the back seat of the car.

"Are you happy?" he asked her.

"Delightfully," she responded and snuggled closer for a quick kiss of assurance.

Anthony drove quickly, speeding as though there wasn't a minute to lose. He pulled into the airport and straight to the plane awaiting their arrival. There wasn't a second to wait as he got out of the car and walked to the side door that Abbie was seated near. He opened it as though he were a chauffeur. Taking her hand and helping her out of the car, he gave her a healthy hug, and said, "Welcome to the family, Abbie."

"Thank you, Anthony. I couldn't be happier. When we get back from our honeymoon, please come and visit."

In Greenwich, early the next morning, they boarded a plane for London. They chose England for their honeymoon because Europe was the music interest of their careers, especially for Charles and his classical background.

Abigail was feeling like a princess again, comparable to Cinderella, except that she was boarding planes rather than riding in horse-driven coaches. The glass slipper was getting more and more comfortable. Reaching England and being escorted from the airport to the hotel in a limousine was a continuation of Charles' wealth and the attention he was showering upon her. She was lost in wonder and romantic love, while also realizing that she had married into wealth and social refinement, which was all so new to her. Her humble background was slowly being pushed away with every luxury and pleasure she was enjoying. Aside from wanting to pinch herself to make sure she was not dreaming, she wondered if this new lifestyle would change her into a less-thankful, less-caring person. Hopefully, it would simply enhance who she was.

The days of their honeymoon were spent seeing every attraction there was in London. The ancient elements of England exposed how young the United States was. Both of their ancestry was in Europe, mostly England. They could sense the attachment, as though the souls of their forefathers were welcoming them.

The highlight of their honeymoon was attending a concert at the Royal Albert Hall. They were delighted when Charles was recognized by a few worldwide fans while walking out of the hall. This unexpected amusement puffed him up enough to desire a return trip someday, perhaps to perform at the Royal Albert Hall in the future.

"I want to come back and play for England, Abbie, and have the London Mozart Symphony Orchestra accompany me," he said, as though it was a providential goal.

"I'm sure that will come someday, darling," she said to him. "You're well-accomplished right now to perform anywhere in the world."

Her faith in his talent was becoming the inspiration of his life and career. His infatuation with romance and England was like a whirlwind of fun that would cool down in time, but her honest acknowledgement of his talent went beyond being in love. When he returned home, he would get Natalie onto the assignment for London. It would take a year, maybe two, but he would be back.

Returning home to Greenwich, Abigail began making the adjustment of accepting a new life away from Bar Harbor and working at making the mansion her own. The desire for something new was fulfilled with the purchase of a cottage to provide a hideaway for them when they had time off together. It would be a perfect place for them to have something together from scratch. Bar Harbor was one of their choices to start searching, but knowing her parents would want to devour their lives while they were there, the decision went to Naugatuck, Connecticut, just an hour-and-a-half drive from Greenwich. No ocean view, but plenty of beautiful trees and foliage. They would look for a small place tucked away from residential areas. The trips from Greenwich would take them across the Housatonic River and close to the celebrated Waterside Clambake Restaurant. It all seemed exciting because stopping to eat at the Clambake would give the trip more enjoyment. Besides, they loved seafood, and this restaurant was known for its inventive seafood menu. It made for a perfect rest stop, especially on Tuesdays when they featured entertainment.

The search for the cottage didn't take long before the right one popped up and stole their hearts. It was a fixer-upper that had two bedrooms with adjoining bathrooms, a large eat-in kitchen with a separate butler's pantry, and an adequate-size living room. It had all the charm of a New England house.

Abigail fell in love with the front porch, planning to buy rattan furniture and imagining them having lunch out there on summer days. She shocked Charles by turning into an interior decorator, having the time of her life selecting furniture, new countertops, and window treatments. Charles contracted the outside work to painters and landscapers. It took five months to complete the project, including the creation of a terrace walkway into the woods behind the property. The best part of their choice for Naugatuck was they didn't need several days off from their schedules to enjoy being there.

They could leave Greenwich early in the morning, drive to Naugatuck, spend the day, and be back home by evening.

Meanwhile, Natalie focused on booking concerts for Charles in the states, while he continued to keep his eye on famous world theaters. His dream was still fanning the flames for playing in Austria, and in Amsterdam, and going back to London. He settled for a booking in California, while Abigail went off to Dallas. Their careers occasionally found them resembling two ships passing in the middle of the night.

Sarah was slowly taking a shine to Abigail, which made life easier for both of them. She was becoming a bit of a mother figure for Abigail, and some days, that's just what was needed, though she didn't like her meddling in things that were her responsibility as Charles' wife. But a special hug coming right out of the blue or compliments after she practiced with Charles at the piano were almost as good as her mother's, and the two of them were beginning to develop a good relationship.

Occasionally, Abigail insisted that Sarah go with them to the cottage, not to cook and clean but to enjoy time away from Greenwich. And this came about when Abigail inquired about Sarah's past life and was saddened to learn that her husband had died before their fifth anniversary. They had no children, so it was understandable that she smothered Charles with her mother-like behavior. She told Abigail about a sister-in-law who lived in Pennsylvania, who never invited anyone to her house or went anywhere. She was a loner and the only relative she had, but she would have nothing to do with Sarah. Abigail thought about what they would do if Sarah got sick and passed away. There would be no one to notify. The more she knew about her, the more she loved her.

Their storybook marriage was new each day, like the infinite consciousness of the soul when it is basking in happiness. They joked about being too happy. Sometimes, Abigail felt afraid because it might be a sin to be so happy. She was like a kid ridding a two-wheel bike. The front wheel might come loose, and the child would crash to the ground. She wondered if it were possible to relax in the truth of Romans 8:28 and believe that all things do keep working together for good.

She and Charles were generally on the same page when it came to important choices and judgments, even religious beliefs. Their conversations never ended in unsettled debates or hurtful arguing. But one day, she brought up questions about the content of their performances. Should they introduce songs of faith more frequently, instead of focusing so much on secular music? Their audiences were basically filled with fans that liked exactly what they were doing. So, the question focused on what would happen to their careers if they started switching boats in the middle of the stream.

"I feel this urge that we should be using our talent for God, not so much for the world," Abigail confided.

That surprised Charles because she was successfully singing an occasional song of faith. That should have satisfied this question. Her audiences loved the "Ave Maria" whenever it was part of her program. They loved "Amazing Grace" and enthusiastically applauded "How Great Thou Art." One of the best audience-pleasers was when she sang Lenny Kravitz's rock song, "Are You Gonna Go My Way?" which appears to cite Jesus and how He didn't leave earth until His work was done. Of course, she toned the tempo down, and it was no surprise that the audience went for it like iced tea on a hot day. This song gave Abigail an opportunity to talk to the audience about the Lord as a way of introducing her faith in Christ Jesus. Abigail would say things to her audience like, "The ultimate Rock Star is Jesus Christ, and God gives choices to us about where to turn." Abigail found she could slip into religious messages easily as long as she kept her pop focus, but she was troubled. Charles had little choice to do anything but what he was doing, unless he left traditional classical standards. His signature pop song at the end of a concert was all he dared do.

"I don't know about trying something new, Abbie," he said in a tone that implied he was not going to change anything.

He had a good point. The highbrow in his audience loved his pop song at the end of each concert, but they were there to hear classical music. He was content to believe that he was doing exactly what he was supposed to do. Write-ups in newspapers and magazines cast him as a conservative, so his followers knew he was not a progressive but a fundamentalist. That was good enough.

They talked it out and ended up feeling confident that their programs were acceptable to God. Charles was wise in issues like this that dealt with right and wrong or liberty verses suppression. He reminded Abbie of I Corinthians 9:22, pointing out that the apostle Paul became all things to all people in his effort to influence others. He became weak to the weak and strong to the strong.

"Perhaps that is how our talents serve the world," he said. "Our fans study our lives and listen to our music. We become them, in a way, and we have an inspiring impact."

Well, if anyone studied Charles' life, Sarah was one of them. She pried into his life with bold curiosity all the time. She couldn't figure out why he was such a happy person and so different from her stiff-necked liberal beliefs about everything, including God. She was a true skeptic, who believed that God kept running tallies on the good and the evil a person did during their lifetime. When they died, she claimed God totaled up both columns. If the good outweighed the bad, you entered Heaven. If not, it was Hell. But being a skeptic, she doubted there was such a place.

One day during one of her inquisitive interrogations, Charles talked with her at length. It was an opportune time to invite her to trust Christ as her Savior, but she would have none of it. Yet it remained obvious that he was influencing her life little by little, and Abigail was there reinforcing his impact. There was an underlying awareness at the Greenwich mansion that lives were being woven into tapestries that were unfinished and yet to be revealed.

Chapter 6

The weather forecast was typical for Greenwich in early July. Today, it would rain, starting in the afternoon and continuing throughout the night. A couple hundred miles offshore, gusty winds were kicking up, but no warnings of anything dangerous heading for Connecticut. No one suspected something was brewing that would be as devastating as the Great Hurricane of 1938 that slammed into Greenwich unsuspectingly.

Early nineteenth-century weather-watchers did not have Doppler, so there was no clue that eighty-mile-per-hour wind gusts and pounding rain were heading toward Greenwich. No hint at all that a large package of Atlantic Ocean water was on its way. The storm back then brought eight inches of rain and a huge tidal wave. After it was over, forecasters named the storm the Yankee Clipper New England Hurricane.

Charles was keeping close watch on the Weather Channel. A few hours into the afternoon, forecasters began warning of near hurricane winds developing in the Bahamas. Computer tracking showed the storm would take a turn toward Greenwich. High winds were predicted, possibly of hurricane strength. There would be floods in some areas.

Rain moved in quickly. By evening, the wind was gusting at high speeds. The storm was not of hurricane force, but the city was plunged into darkness as power went out. A gas generator kept the lights and the appliances running at Charles' place. Local television channels reported heavy traffic tie-ups on the main streets, caused from numerous downed tree limbs. People were advised to stay inside.

Anxious to view his property, Charles turned on the outside lights and stepped out to check the trees in the terrace garden and look for damage on the glassed-in swimming pool. The wind was extremely strong, but he saw no damage. On his way back inside, a strong gust of wind caught the door. Before Charles could grab hold of it, the gust slammed the door hard against his right hand, crushing it into the doorjamb. Pain shot up his arm. He hollered for Abigail, while struggling to hold the door open and get inside. His hand felt like it had been hit with a sledgehammer.

He was groaning with pain when Abigail reached him. She saw he was favoring his right hand and breathing heavily, as though pain was taking away his breath. Hurrying him into the kitchen and to the sink, she began running cold water over his hand. The ring finger and the little finger were disfigured, almost flattened from the knuckle to the fingertips.

Sarah ran into the kitchen when she heard the commotion and took over as though she was Florence Nightingale.

"Let's get some ice on that," she said, grabbing a plastic bag out of the drawer and filling it with ice cubes. She placed the bag on the palm of his hand, noticing that his fingers looked mutilated. She grabbed a clean tea towel and wrapped it loosely around his hand and the ice, all the time holding back the agony she felt for him.

"This looks bad, Mr. Ricci. I think you should go to the ER," she said.

"We will never get through the dark streets," he groaned. "There's too many trees down. It's too dangerous to go outside right now. I'll be okay. The ice will help. I can see about it in the morning when it's light."

It was midnight when the winds were quiet again. The storm passed, but Charles was battling the worst pain of his life. His hand had swelled to twice its size, and two fingers looked deformed. Fear of losing his career was starting to move into his mind, but he kept the horrible thought to himself. He allowed Abigail to help him take his clothes off so he could get into bed. The Extra Strength Tylenol was helping to curb the pain, but the agony over his damaged fingers was tormenting him. Would he play the piano again?

"Darling, I am hurting right along with you," Abigail said, kissing his forehead and adjusting the pillow under his head. "As soon as daylight comes, I'll drive you to the hospital. We'll find our way through the mess out there. Don't worry. We'll get help. Now, try to sleep."

All those orders sounded like an army sergeant. Don't worry. Try to sleep. How could he sleep and not worry when his hand was throbbing with pain and his life's ambition might be down the drain?

She slipped into bed beside him. The fear he saw in her eyes told him that she was asking the same questions. What would he do if the bones were crushed and the hand was permanently crippled? Would he have to give up playing the piano? Neither of them would talk about it.

The drive to the hospital was like finding a way through a maze of broken limbs and fallen trees. The twenty-minute trip took an hour.

Abigail stayed with Charles in the ER unit, waiting for someone to take him for x-rays. It seemed like an eternity before an attendant came. Another eternity before he was wheeled back to the unit, and then another wait for a doctor's report. Meanwhile, Charles was being recognized by some fans. Several doctors stopped by to greet him and to let him know they had downloaded his music. One intern mentioned that he had attended one of his performances in California while on vacation. All these fans were well-meaning, but Charles was too concerned about his hand to be thrilled that people were recognizing him. Finally, a doctor came into the unit.

"You have a lot of damage in those fingers," the doctor said, while he pulled the curtain around the unit to give privacy.

Charles became more anxious. The sight of the curtain being pulled around his unit scared him as much as the look on the doctor's face.

"The knuckles of two fingers are severely crushed, as you can see with the irregularity of their alignment. The rest of the hand looks good, just bruising and swelling that will correct on its own. Surgery is needed to repair the crushed knuckles. I'll give you a list of orthopedic surgeons here in the area."

Charles reached for Abigail's hand and then asked the doctor, "How bad does it look? I'm a pianist."

The doctor shrugged. It was obvious that he didn't want to get involved with presuming good or bad or making false promises. He avoided a direct answer.

"Look through the list," he said, "and do some research on your own. Don't waste time. You need to get after this right away."

The nurse wrapped his hand in gauze and secured it with tape, making small talk while she worked. She left and then came back with the list of local surgeons and a cloth sling.

"You need to keep your hand elevated above your waist," she said while she adjusted the sling over his shoulder. He didn't need that instruction. He already knew it was more comfortable to hold his hand up because when the blood rushed into it, it hurt worse.

She gave him the verbal instructions everyone gets before leaving the ER and a prescription for pain pills. Charles couldn't wait to get home and start making calls. He was frantic to find a surgeon.

Abigail was as desperate to get help as he was. She called Ellie and Marco and her parents on the way home from the hospital, using the Bluetooth so she could continue driving. Charles kept interrupting, explaining what had happened and blurting out that he was fearful about not being able to play the piano once he had the surgery. Panic overtook the entire family as though lightning had suddenly struck.

Marco immediately went into his office at the penthouse and started a computer search for skilled surgeons. Charles searched on the internet as soon as he got home but was slow as a snail without the use of his right hand. Picking at keys with his left fingers and bobbing his head up and down from the keyboard to the screen was frustrating. Abigail wasted no time searching on her notebook computer and hurriedly making side notes to take to Charles. Sarah was tending to their need to eat and doing small things that helped to calm things down. Back in New York, Ellie was calling friends to get a prayer chain started. In Bar Harbor, Irene and Rod were getting things ready to travel to wherever the surgery would be done.

It was barely thirty minutes later when Marco found a surgeon in Cleveland who was rated as one of the top ten orthopedic surgeons in the nation. He quickly called Charles.

"This surgeon is at the top of the list countrywide," he said. "I'll email his credentials to you. That is, if you and Abigail haven't found a surgeon that beats his qualifications. Let me know, and I'll call and get you an appointment, since I've already talked to them. They understand the situation and know it's an emergency. I'll fly you to Cleveland. We'll get you there in no time."

Everything was running as fast as lightning.

The phone was on speaker, and Abigail quickly nodded yes to Charles.

"Dad," Charles said, "go ahead and call him. We'll get in the car right now. We can be at the penthouse in an hour. I'll keep in touch with you along the way."

Sarah helped pack a few things and shoved some snacks into a bag. In no time, they were pulling out of the garage, ready to maneuver through the maze of downed trees once again and drive through deep water, heading for New York.

As if they all had hotlines to Heaven and God had no one else to save or heal, things started moving quickly. Charles was in Cleveland and prepped for surgery in less than forty-eight hours. The surgeon was very solemn about the injury and talked frankly to Charles in the presence of the family. He would do what he could but made no promises.

"I won't know how badly the bones are crushed until I can get in there. And there could also be nerve damage, which will cause permanent numbness."

There was nothing encouraging coming from this noted surgeon, who would carefully take Charles' crippled fingers into his skilled hands and work to get them moving. Emotions and questions were engulfing everyone's minds. Why did this happen? Shouldn't God have stopped the freak wind that slammed the door? Was this accident deserved? Was it an act of punishment from God?

The OR attendant rolled the gurney into the room. Everyone quickly said whatever they thought would encourage Charles and moved out of the way. Abigail kissed him and noticed that the look on his face was like that of a soldier ready for war. He certainly was in a great battle, and if his face told the story, he was ready to fight with all his might.

"I love you," Abigail said touching his face. "I'll be praying."

"I love you, too, sweetheart," he answered.

The gurney rolled down the long hallway toward the OR elevators.

******

Marco turned and looked at Abigail and said, "It's up to God."

She was white with fear, and in compassion, he moved close and took her into his arms. She could hold in her emotions no longer and wept as though her heart were breaking.

Marco gathered the family into a circle at the foot of the empty hospital bed and prayed.

It was three hours later when the surgeon walked into the surgical waiting room, green scrubs and cap still on and a look that was not encouraging. He was carrying a clipboard.

He focused mostly on Abigail while he gave his report and drew diagrams.

"The breaks in the ring finger and fifth finger were clean fractures and should heal well. The second knuckle of the index finger and the third knuckle of the middle finger were badly crushed. I did what I could to reconstruct both knuckles. If they heal well, he will be able to bend them as before. The nerve damage is the most concerning. It may be that he will lose feeling in both those fingers. Time will tell."

"How long will his fingers be cast or wrapped, and how long before feeling returns, if the nerves healed?" asked Abigail anxiously.

"His fingers will stay wrapped with splints for about six weeks; after that time, he will need extensive therapy to strengthen the hand and get the knuckles bending again. It may be three months or more before he has any feeling if the nerves heal correctly. The possibility remains that the fingers will be numb.

"He will be out of recovery soon. A nurse will call you when he's awake and back in a room. I want him to spend one night here, and if everything looks good, he can go home tomorrow."

Ellie suggested they go to the coffee shop at the other end of the hospital and get a bite to eat.

"We'll sign out, and they can page us when he's back in the room."

Hungry, tired, and drained emotionally, each of them went through the line and got their food. They squeezed in tightly at a small table. Ellie gave the prayer of thanksgiving. They ate and waited.

******

Walking along the beach of Long Island Sound was the only thing Charles could do without difficulty. Trying to hold a fork and eat with one good finger and a thumb was difficult. He was right-handed, so switching to the left wasn't any better. Cutting meat was impossible, but he mastered pulling on socks with his left hand. He was a good sport about every difficulty, never complaining, always taking an optimistic view of his new disabilities that he hoped were temporary. The wrapping was no longer on his fingers, and a therapist came three days a week to help him exercise. There was no feeling in the tips of both injured fingers. Moving the knuckles was accomplished only with the help of his left hand, moving them as far as range of motion allowed. Four times a day, he faithfully did the exercises, hoping that movement and feeling would return.

He felt lonely away from the piano but was holding up fairly well, and his warrior's determination was evident. His faith was strong that God would bring healing, but he still feared he would never play again. Strange how fear and faith go together.

Abigail was leaving in a few days for Boston to perform at the Boston Sympathy Hall, hoping that Charles would go with her.

"Come with me, Charlie," she begged, while knowing he likely would say no. But she had to ask because she hated to leave him while he was still stressful and cooped-up. Furthermore, coaxing him back into the theater atmosphere might help encourage him.

It was no big deal for both of them to fly to Boston. Whenever she was booked there, it required three days and two nights. She knew the routine. Rehearsal the day before the evening show and leisure time the morning of the performance. It would be ideal if Charles was with her. If nothing else, he could stand in as her coach during rehearsals and feel useful.

"I don't think so, Abbie," he replied with an air of burden.

Immediately, she switched into her famous *I'm not taking no for an answer* role.

"Charlie, I need you to come with me because I've read some disturbing things about the orchestra conductor being a beastly brute. I really need your support. He's known to demand all sorts of impossible things of the artists, and he has no patience. I want you with me as my coach."

He swallowed her plea hook, line, and sinker. Putting it the way she did gave him little chance to come up with a good excuse to stay home. On the same token, it wasn't like him to play the martyr—to be the poor, unfortunate person wallowing in self-pity while she went off to do what she loved doing. Still, he wasn't sure how he would feel, sitting in the audience knowing that he might never be on stage again. He was greatly tempted to stay home. The problem was that he didn't know if he could graciously manage the agony of defeat and ignore his feelings while he sat watching her perform. The bottom line of his decision came down to the fact that he knew his place was to support her. After all, her unselfish support for him had been in constant motion since his accident.

He walked into another room, leaving her with no answer.

Then he returned.

"Okay, Abbie, I'll go," he said. "Call Natalie and ask her to get the airline tickets."

They both had performed at the Boston Symphony Hall, so this was no problem as far as being familiar with the auditorium and the area of Boston. Managing the narcissistic conductor would come easier with Charles acting as Abigail's coach. It was the audience that was the big deal. Her desire was to make them love her while she gave them her very best. The program director had her scheduled to go on stage last, which meant her performance was the main attraction. She was the star player. She would sing five songs. The pick for her faith song was "Angels Calling," a heart-wrenching song made famous by The Tenors. It would serve her heart's desire to bring something of deep value to her audience. The last song would be the ballad "Time," a well-celebrated song performed years ago by Enya, the beautiful Irish singer.

The hall was packed. Charles was sitting center-front, four rows back, and in good sight of Abigail. The lights on stage permitted her to see him as well. She was excited and nervous. Tonight seemed special for some reason, even though Charles had often been in her audience.

Her fans were enthusiastic, loving every song. The lights changed on stage to a soft blue for the faith song, and Abigail moved to center stage and stepped up to a floor mic. A forty-voice female choir took their place at the left of the stage to sing the background.

The orchestra played the introduction, and "Angels Calling" began to fill the air. The words flowed powerfully throughout the auditorium with sacred meaning for anyone who had said a final goodbye to a loved one. Abigail was aware of the sensitivity of the song, so no surprise as she looked across the audience to see many people wiping their eyes. The words filled the air with melodious sweetness. Abigail's beautiful soprano voice singing the words, *"Don't cry . . . / Can't you hear the angels calling me up . . . / You will be in my heart forever . . ."*[4]

******

Charles was moved with emotion as thoughts of his mother, Katie, came to him. The words brought back hidden feelings. Abigail

---

4   The Tenors, "Angels Calling," *Under One Sky*, No. 7, Universal, 2015, CD.

filled the deep hole in his heart that the death of his mother caused, but for the moment, Katie was there, speaking those words to him. He choked back tears and wished he could someday play that song for his father with Abigail singing the lyrics.

There was a brief pause. The orchestra played while Abigail hurried off-stage and slipped into a different gown for the last two songs. Her dress was a white, polyester, floor-length sheath that packs in a suitcase wrinkle-free. It was her favorite dress, and it highlighted her hourglass figure and dark hair. The audience broke into enthusiastic applause as she re-entered the stage, taking her place at the side of a grand piano. She glanced into the audience, holding the hand mic down, searching for Charles during the introduction. She spotted him. He glowed with a smile that thrilled her heart.

Her last song was choreographed with special spotlights that shown only on her and dimmed the orchestra behind. For this number, she again stood in the center of the stage but as far forward as possible. This was a new ballad for her audience, and she wanted to sing it intimately. Close, as though she might reach out and touch them.

The floor mic was in position; the spotlights were beaming down on her; and the introduction began. The audience was beyond ready to hear the song, "Only Time."

No sooner had she begun to sing, then her fans started applauding.

More smooth and sugary than the Irish singer, Enya, who had made the song famous years ago, Abigail's voice filled the auditorium, and the message of the song was born again. Like the birth of the blues, the melody was mesmerizing. The lyrics asked every lover's questions and conveyed every lonely person's wonder.

******

During the rehearsal, she was intense and had no recognition of how those words rang true for her, but now they came alive while she sang to her audience. Indeed, the words were true. In the right time, she had met him. In the deep longings of her soul, her heart sighed. In her worry for Charles' acceptance, she cried. Neither time nor love gave the answers.

******

She wasn't the only one moved. Charles felt a tenderness toward her that he had never experienced before. In every song she performed that night, he saw a woman emerge with an extraordinary gift that was far beyond words to adequately describe. It was as though he was seeing her in a new perspective, a woman who recognized her gift and used it perfectly. She owned her audience. They loved and wanted her. In this tremendous realm of popularity, he felt that she far surpassed him. For the moment, it didn't matter to him if he never played again. She would go on, regardless. She was a star. He couldn't wait to get backstage and tell her how wonderful she was.

As faithful as the sun coming up every morning, Charles continued working with his injured fingers, straining to move them and massaging them as taught to him by his therapist. Months passed with no movement returning to his knuckles. X-rays revealed the fractures and the repair on the knuckles healed well, but the final outcome was waiting to be known. The stiffness was defiant, as though it would never give up. The feeling in the fingertips was slowly coming back, but full recovery remained guarded.

Despair was starting to set in. Occasionally, he sat at the piano, playing a tune with his left hand, constructing melodious cords with his five good fingers. Now and then, he put the right hand to the keys, straining to make them play the notes, but it was useless. They would not cooperate. The gift God gave him was still there, in his heart and in his soul, but his knuckles stayed stiff, as though they were fastened in a stronghold that the minions of Satan had control over.

He would soon lose his audience and his honored place of esteem in the theaters if he didn't start performing. While the days tediously went by, reality was closing in, and panic was taunting him. The dream of playing at the Musikverein Hall in Vienna or at Concertgebouw in Amsterdam was getting away from him. He should forget about playing in London at the Royal Albert Hall. His piano-playing days were ending. He needed a miracle.

Chapter 7

An idea was incubating in Charles' mind. The notion that if he could not play the piano, he could write music. He needed to do something with his life, or he would wither and die. Writing music would never take the place of performing for an audience, but it was better than nothing. He wasn't thinking of just writing a song or two but of creating an entire concerto. In the middle of the night, he often awoke, and the music was there, playing in his mind, teasing him, daring him to write what he was hearing. He would get up and go to the music room and jot down the melody, while it was still dancing in his brain.

The first musical movements of the concerto were completed with so much joy that he wanted to spend every waking moment on it. He was secretly working, hiding it from Abigail because he wasn't sure he could finish the project or that he was even talented enough to undertake such a thing. But regardless, he was into it like a hungry kid eating a Snickers bar. How silly it seemed that he was tucking his work in the storage compartment of the piano bench. Of all the people in the world who would encourage this project, it would be Abigail, but he was hiding it as though it was a stray kitten he had snuck into the house. One day, he could keep it to himself no longer and let it out of the bag.

"If I cannot play, I must write," he said flat out to her. "I'm composing a concerto."

He said this as though he were confessing a sin.

"Well, I think that's a great idea," Abigail responded, as though he had revealed something that she had been thinking.

"To be honest, I was thinking about the same thing the other day," she continued. "I said to myself, if Charlie can't play the piano, he can write music. But I was hesitant to mention this to you because I know how desperately you want to play for an audience."

He smiled as though getting it out in the open and having her blessing was like removing an elephant off his shoulders.

"Two brilliant minds always work together," he said and then laughed.

Days and weeks went by, and he established a regular routine for his work. As soon as breakfast was finished, he went to the piano with paper and pencil, playing notes and chords with his left hand while struggling with his right hand to jot the notes down. It was a difficult task trying to use his right thumb and two defiant fingers to cooperate together and write the notes. There were frustrations and many erasures. But his obsession with this project kept him going no matter how difficult it was to scribble notes with his crippled right hand.

Abigail knew that Charles' preoccupation to sit at the piano day after day writing a concerto came from his passion to perform again. Watching him struggle to play notes and write with such difficulty was heartbreaking, but she would never mention how sad it made her. She often stood in the archway of the music room and listened, without him noticing.

"Abbie, come here and sit with me," he said one day when he caught her listening. "I want you to hear this part."

As though he were teaching her about the strings of the piano and the music in his soul, he explained how the development of the concerto was capturing the theme of an eagle in flight.

"Listen, Abbie, these few bars of the piece mimic the beauty of a graceful bird soaring high in the air. He played with his left hand and occasionally hit a note with his right index finger to give a hint of what the right hand should be doing.

She was mesmerized with the sound and easily visualized the flight of a beautiful bird soaring upward, then swooping down close to the ground, and then gracefully bursting into a glorious flush that kept it climbing even higher.

"Oh, Charlie, it's beautiful. Someday, you will play it for me with both hands. I know you will."

Seeing him work so hard made her heart break again and again for him. She saw his enormous talent and knew that he would give anything to play his concerto with both hands. He wasn't fooling her one bit, hiding his disappointment.

He announced one day that the concerto was finished.

"I need to transpose it onto a clean copy and have Natalie take it to the printer. What shall we name it, Abbie?"

"I'm not sure, but I believe a popular word for a concerto is *canticle*. Maybe name it 'Canticle of the Birds.'"

He didn't like the word *canticle*. His audience was sophisticated, but not truly highbrow or scholarly. "I think canticle is too academic. What if we drop the words concerto and canticle and title it 'Flight of the Birds'?"

Abigail thought for a moment and liked it.

"It has a classical flair, and it's simple. When the concerto is played with both hands, the flight of a bird will be visualized by the audience. I could see a bird gracefully flying when you played that one part for me."

"Well, that settles it," Charles said. "'Flight of the Birds' it will be."

******

Abigail put on a bathing suit, threw a coverall loosely over her shoulders, and walked into the terrace garden where Charles was sitting.

"Come on, Charlie," she said in a cheerful voice, as though he had to immediately get out of the chair, or else, she would pull him out.

"Swim with me!

"Oh, Abbie, I'm not in the mood right now," he grumbled.

But not taking no for an answer, she grabbed his arms and proceeded to pull him out of the chair.

"Don't be a spoil sport," she nagged.

She had a genius way of getting what she wanted, and he knew if he didn't get up and find a swimsuit in the bathhouse, she would continue to pester the daylights out of him.

Patiently, she waited for him, dog-paddling in the water to stay afloat. When he appeared in a swimsuit, walking slow and dragging a towel behind him, she called for him to hurry up, and then swam off into the deep end of the pool. Determined that she would not coax him into a race, he dove in and swam in the opposite direction, heading toward the sauna pool, where he preferred to relax.

The sauna water was warm and soothing. He had to admit he was glad to get up out of the chair. He faced her direction and relaxed with his arms stretched over the tiled edge and watched her dive off the board in a perfect bullet position.

Cutting into the water with very little splash, she was like a beautiful dolphin. But just as she came up to the surface of the water, the muscle in one of her legs went into a painful, grabbing cramp. She struggled, trying to swim to the edge of the pool and grab onto the side ladder, but her leg was pulling her down. She screamed for Charles.

At first, he thought she was kidding. She was always full of life, and this was like her to play a prank. But then she went under and came back up, screaming for help, and he knew she was in trouble. He jumped out of the sauna in lightning speed and ran the length of the pool where she was struggling and going down for the second time. He dove in and grabbed hold of her, turning her in an upward position so she could breathe. He yelled at her to stop fighting and held her tight while he swam to the side ladder.

She was choking and coughing to get the water out of her lungs.

"Here, grab onto the ladder." he told her, while getting behind her to boost her up.

"I don't think I can get up there; my leg is in a terrible cramp," she cried hysterically.

"You can make it!" he said firmly. "Use your good leg. Grab the side of the pool as soon as I get you up there!"

He was holding onto the ladder with his right hand, and with his left hand, he started pushing her upward with all the strength he had. She was up over the edge and out of the pool in no time, rubbing the calf of her leg and groaning with pain.

As soon as he climbed up the ladder and got to her, he started massaging the muscle to help loosen the cramp.

"It's easing now, Charlie," she said, running both hands up and down her leg.

"Are you okay, now?" he asked, helping her rub her leg again, as though nothing mattered but saving her from drowning.

"Yes, thank God you were here," she said.

Then she looked down at her leg and noticed while he was massaging the muscle that the two stiff knuckles of his right hand were bending perfectly.

"Charlie!" she gasped. "Your knuckles are bending! Look!"

He had not noticed anything while saving her life. He held his hand up and opened and closed it, watching the knuckles move as though they had never been hurt. He kept opening and closing his hand. It was amazing. Excitement grabbed hold of both of them as though God was standing right there, saying, "Look what I've done for you!" They shouted and hollered with happiness, so loud that Sarah heard it in the kitchen and came running to see what was happening.

When she got there, both of them were dancing and hollering as though they were walking on fire ants. They looked like two drunk clowns in a circus.

"What in the world is going on?" Sarah asked.

"Charles' knuckles are bending!" Abigail cried. She grabbed his hand and shoved it over toward her.

"Look! They're bending!"

"Oh, my goodness, they are!" Sarah said as though she couldn't figure out how it had happened.

Charles started from the beginning, telling her that Abigail dove into the water and got a leg cramp and almost drowned.

"I guess my knuckles got forced really hard when I was boosting her up the ladder. I wasn't noticing what I was doing. My right hand was gripping the ladder. All I was aware of was getting her out of the water. She would have drowned if I hadn't been here."

"Wow," Sarah remarked while she felt Charles' knuckles and watched him bend them. "I guess miracles can happen anywhere, even in a swimming pool."

Without any further ado, they dressed, and Charles went into the music room. An audience of two followed him, curious to see what he was going to do. Truly, it was an anxious moment.

He sat at the piano and hesitated, looking at the keys, feeling full of excitement and nervous as a little boy up to bat for the first time. He started vigorously exercising his right hand, opening and shutting it. All the knuckles were still bending without pain. He thought for a moment about what he would play, and then it came to him—the old hymn, "Great Is Thy Faithfulness." He knew it by heart. He placed his fingers at the keyboard and began. He played effortlessly with feeling and perfect precision, giving the notes expression.

As he finished the seven bars of the hymn, Abigail walked to the piano; and without any necessary cue, Charles played the song again, and she sang the lyrics that clearly expressed the mercy and faithfulness of God's love.

When she finished singing, he looked over at Sarah and saw her crying. Sarah's tears caught onto Abigail's joyful emotions, and she started crying along with her. What a scene of triumph in the music room! Charles simply sat back and let the two women cry. *Help yourself; I know just what you're feeling.* The miracle he had hoped for had come, and he was thankful and ready to take on the world.

But then, as though a lightbulb went off in his brain, he quickly grabbed his concerto and began to play what he had struggled for weeks to create. He played as though he had practiced it a hundred times. The melody captured all of them. But Charles was especially moved in a swirl of sensations that associated with the accomplishment of listening to it in its fullness for the first time. It was every bit the likeness of the title, "Flight of the Birds." The melody gave perfect imagery of birds in flight patterns, flying over treetops or making their trip to the south in the winter. There were fortes of expression and then softness. The accents Charles gave the piece teased the imagination as well as giving pleasure in listening.

When the concerto ended, he sat motionless, staring at his right hand. It seemed he had come out of a bad dream in which an enemy was pursuing him. In the dream, he stumbled, and the enemy grabbed hold of him and held him captive in a prison of darkness and despair. But he awoke to find himself freed.

Abigail walked to him while he remained seated. She put her arms around him and said, "See, I said you would play the concerto with both hands someday."

As the excitement of this miracle moment continued, he found himself calling Marco to give him the good news.

"Dad, you'll never guess what has happened," he said with the most enthusiastic joy his vocal cords could deliver.

"What's that?" Marco asked, putting the speaker on and motioning for Ellie to listen.

He began the whole story, from beginning to end, even relating that he originally didn't want to get into the pool. The conversation ended with Aunt Ellie butting in and insisting he come to the penthouse so she could hear him play. No better place than there, at the grand piano Charles learned to play as a young boy.

"We'll have a party and celebrate," she declared.

"Aunt Ellie," Charles broke in, "you remind me of Uncle Charley. He never let a good thing rest. He was always planning celebrations. I don't know if I want a big celebration. I'm simply thankful I can play again."

"Nonsense!" Ellie said. "We're going to have a family celebration, and I won't take no for an answer."

Ellie settled that quick, and Charles didn't get off the phone until a date was settled upon. Now it was Abigail's time to call her parents and give them the good news. It seemed that the whole world should know and celebrate with them.

"Oh please, come to New York and meet us at the penthouse," she persuaded. "It won't be a family circle if you're not there. Mom and Dad, you're coming, and that's it. I'll make the arrangements!"

It was only a few days later that Natalie got a performance booked for Charles at the Meyerson Center in Dallas. This was the beginning of getting back into the limelight and performing again on a steady schedule.

"Now, what about the concerto?" she questioned, knowing that it was printed, and the copyright was secure. "It might be a good idea if we sent it off to a conductor in London."

Charles was far ahead of her with that thought. He had decided while still composing the piece that he wanted to present it first to Henry Rosenbaum, conductor of the London Core Symphony Orchestra. If he were honored to play it anywhere, London would be his choice, and Rosenbaum would be the conductor to accommodate the piano performance.

"Natalie, that's a great thought," he said, letting her think she came up with it on her own. "Get the phone number of Rosenbaum. I'll call first, and if he will agree to look at it, you can send it."

The world was opening back up for Charles and Abigail. Their storybook marriage was back on track.

Chapter 8

No one would question that Charles loved Abigail and that he loved his mansion in Greenwich and the cottage in Naugatuck. Still, he missed his family and the theaters and the parties in New York. He often reminisced his dad going all out for his clients in Texas and Colorado, renting limousines to bring them from the LaGuardia Airport to the penthouse. He remembered his mother and Ellie having everything perfect the moment the guests stepped off the elevators and into the great room. Everything about New York and the penthouse was still happily recollected in his mind. The food served on the terrace, the music, the noise and laughter. Even hearing the stories of Uncle Charley, who died before he was born, was a happy memory. He was named after Uncle Charley, and everyone said he was just like him. Well, except for the Cuban cigars he smoked and the martinis he drank, which Aunt Ellie continually scolded him about.

Psychologists say nostalgia is good because it makes people feel socially connected, like the happiness of visiting a long-lost friend or being with a group of friends you haven't seen for years. Funny how the past often seems more positive than the present. Charles had these nostalgic feelings entertaining his mind frequently. So, when his Aunt Ellie suggested they celebrate the miraculous healing of his right hand, he was happy to join his family and friends and make a big thing of it. He also loved showcasing Abigail at every opportunity, watching how people stared at her because she was beautiful and talented. He was proud that she belonged to him.

No one was left out of this celebration, including Abigail's parents. Marco was determined to get them to New York without any trouble or expense that might give them an excuse not to come. He planned to transport them to New York in the company jet and insisted they spend a few days before going back home. To make the party even more exciting, he invited several of his first-rate clients from Colorado—those who know Charles well.

Of course, it never failed that Ellie spared nothing to make parties a grand event, and she warned Charles ahead of time that he would be playing the piano for them.

"The people from Colorado know how serious your accident was and understand that you were in jeopardy of losing your career. So, you must play for them," she told him. Then she added another pressure. "Many of them have not met Abigail, so I hope she will sing at least one song."

He would play all right, but knowing this mainstream group from Colorado, he would not subject them to his concerto, "Flight of the Birds." He would gladly take their requests, and if he knew the song, he would play it. If Abigail agreed to sing, he would accompany her on the piano. Aunt Ellie surely would get her way.

As soon as the buffet dinner was over, Anthony and Joe removed the tables from the terrace and revved up the electronic music system. In no time, the dancing began, and the party was getting on. Those who didn't want to dance mulled around in the great room, talking, and nibbling on left-over snacks.

Ellie was truly bothered about the things she had no control over and seriously gave them to Marco to keep order and police the type of dancing. The crowd from Colorado was lively and full of fun. The fun and noise could get carried away, just like old times when Uncle Charley was in charge.

The whole shebang of things was turning into a grand event. Twenty-five people, and all of them in a party mood—most of them progressive and not practicing the Christian faith. Well, maybe not so much for Irene and Rod because they were basically abiding with the precepts of the Bible and very quiet. Abigail would give Charles the "eye" if she thought they needed someone to strike up a conversation with them. But at the Ricci's penthouse, never underestimate the power of influence when a crowd of cheerful people are celebrating. Before the evening was over, Rod and Irene were dancing on the terrace.

In a grand exhibit to show how well his right hand was working and to keep the party mood going, Charles played "The Flight of the Bumble Bee." He was grandstanding, of course; but he had good reason, and they loved it.

Who could follow Charles, unless it would be Abigail, coaxed by Ellie to step up and sing? And wouldn't you know, there just happened to be a sound track of Kelly Clarkson's song "I Dare You" waiting to be loaded into the system. It was useless to wiggle out of it, not when she had just recently added that popular hit to her performance repertoire.

What an awesome show of singing talent she made to the Colorado gang with that song. They were almost on their knees begging her to sing more. But that was all they got from her.

"Thank you so much," Abigail said as she did a half-bow and walked over to Charles. "That's all for tonight. Maybe another time."

At that point, Marco wasn't ready to let the party dry up. He rushed over to the piano, eager to show off a little of his talent, which most everyone was well acquainted with. But he was a happy exhibitionist, just like his late brother-in-law, Charley. He sat down on the piano bench and looked over at Abigail and asked her if she knew the words to "I've Got Rhythm."

"Maybe some of them," she responded, wondering what her overly excited father-in-law was up to.

"Come on then; get over here and sing what you know and make up the rest," he coaxed.

It turned into hilarious karaoke when Abigail stumbled over the words and started making up goofy lyrics, laughing so hard she could not continue. One by one, others got up and stood at the piano, singing whatever Marco played and deliberately messing up the lyrics. They resembled a group of adults turning into silly kids. Marco played into the night, and there was a steady stream of singers shrieking out the most insane lyrics to popular songs and having a ball. The fun didn't stop until well after midnight, when everyone got worn down.

******

Charles was sitting on top of the world when out of the blue, good news came, landing an invitation for him to perform at the Sydney Opera House in New South Wales, Australia. This invitation would certainly boost his career to the top and possibly set him up to perform at the Musikverein Hall in Vienna. The door was wide open for him to accept this booking because he had not yet heard from Henry Rosenbaum in London regarding his concerto. The only problem with Australia was the timing for Abigail. She was booked at the Paramont Theater in Austin, Texas, at the same time.

The Paramont Theater was in no way comparable to the Sydney Opera House, but it was very posh and profitable enough for her career. The old building had class and carried an impressive list of past performers. Seating capacity was over two thousand. She was hooked and especially committed after learning that seats were almost sold out. She would perform one night only, but it was the next day after Charles would be in Sydney.

"I want to be with you so bad it hurts," she told him.

He understood her disappointment. In fact, he was fighting his feelings just as hard, but when a booking was made in the entertainment world, it was next to impossible to wiggle out of.

"I'd give anything to have you with me, Abbie," he said, hugging her.

"Tell you what," he continued, with an idea that suddenly popped into his head. "When you get back from Austin, drive up to the cottage, and I'll meet you there as soon as I get back. Let's take some time off, just you and me."

His plan smoothed the disappointment a little, but not being together in Sydney was a real bummer. Of all the people sitting in the audience, she was his prized fan.

Australians are incredibly friendly people. It's like the U.K. in many respects because the people have much in common with Britain. They seem to be closely aligned, even being thousands of miles apart. The territory is surrounded by four different seas, which explains the massive sun worshiping at the beaches. But Charles would have no time to bask in the sun, not with two days of afternoon performances and four evening performances. He would do well to rest in his hotel room and maybe do some shopping for Abigail.

When he stepped off the plane, he went immediately to the Sydney Opera House by limousine to meet the directors. The sight of the city was everything he imagined it would be. Seeing the opera house for the first time, he understood why it was one of the most photographed buildings in the world. The gleaming white, sail-shaped shells of the roof were spectacular. He snapped photos and sent them to Abigail, with videos as well, telling her how magnificent South Wales was. He was amazed to discover the number of rooms in the opera house, one thousand in all. And there was no problem finding a place to eat and shop in his spare time. The house had four restaurants and several souvenir shops.

There was one disappointment for him, however, when he practiced his performance. The acoustics in the hall lacked power. The ceiling was built so high that sound could not be captured and radiated like it is in smaller theaters. The managers and directors were sensitive to this problem and did their best to get the sound system tweaked to his preferences. The orchestra conductor was also conscious of the sound problem and worked to keep the instruments soft, to create an advantage for the piano to have the widest range of acoustics.

Standing back stage before the program started, Charles looked at his once-crippled fingers and brought them softly into the other hand, as though to feel them and love them and know again that he was there in this magnificent theater because of a loving God. *Thank you, Lord*, he silently prayed. *This evening belongs to You.*

Taking a deep breath as the curtain went up, he slowly walked on stage and toward the piano that was placed center-stage. The crowd cheered and clapped. Even a few hoots came from the back of the theater. He bowed and then took his position at the piano. The crowd's enthusiasm electrified him, and all that mattered in this jubilant moment was to play his best and please them.

At the end of his performance, two standing ovations and cries for more kept him on stage for one more pop song. He reached back in time to the 1950s and played "Moonglow," the theme from the movie *Picnic*. By far, he was better than the pianist who played this song in the Benny Goodman Quartet years ago. The curtain then came down for the last time, and Charles was quickly driven to his hotel. Despite the sixteen-hour time difference in the U.S., he called Abigail to wake her and tell her that his audience was wonderful and that he had just experienced one of the most fabulous performances of his career.

"Oh, darling, that's wonderful," she said with a yawn. "I knew Sydney would love you."

"They seemed to, but not as much as I love you and miss you," he responded.

"Miss you too and can't wait to see you."

Charles turned off his phone and stretched across the bed, too tired to get into pajamas.

******

Abigail's performance in Austin was truly rewarding, even knowing that Charles was thousands of miles away. The theater was packed with fans, and the audience was warm and wonderful toward her. She finished her performance and was back home in Greenwich in twenty-four hours. She made a quick call to Charles, saying that she was heading for their cottage the next morning.

At daybreak, she packed a few clothes while Sarah gathered food items into a large picnic basket. There would be no need for her to stop at the grocery store before arriving at the cottage. With everything packed, she bid Sarah goodbye and started out.

"Take care and drive safely," Sarah said, waving goodbye as Abigail drove off.

The morning was perfect for driving. There wasn't a cloud in the sky. It would be lunchtime when she crossed the Housatonic River, and the perfect place to stop for lunch was at the Waterside Clambake Restaurant. It would be lonely eating without Charles, but they were friends with the owners after eating there so many times, and that would make the stop more pleasant. She settled back into the driver's seat and turned Sirius Satellite Radio to her favorite channel.

Much of the trip was on a two-lane highway. She knew it well, like the back of her hand. Occasionally, a passing lane would pop up for a couple of miles, which came in handy if stuck behind a slow-moving truck or an elderly granny driving at a snail's pace.

The soft song "My Heart at Thy Sweet Voice" from the musical *Samson and Delilah* was playing. Abigail relaxed into it, and without realizing, she dozed off and veered over the yellow line, clipping the back of a car going in the opposite direction. The impact shoved the car enough to tip it, and it rolled.

Suddenly, Abigail was upside down, looking at the ceiling of the car. Her heart was pounding like a drum keeping fast rhythm, and she was twisted like a pretzel in the car seat.

"Oh, dear God, help me," she cried out loud. "Please, please help me!"

Panic swept through her. It was strange that she didn't feel pain—she didn't even notice that—but being trapped in the car was creating claustrophobic fear. She had to get out of there. She tried to squirm and lift herself out of the seat, but she couldn't move. She lost consciousness.

It was several minutes before EMS got there, and another forty-five minutes before she was air-lifted to a hospital in Waterbury. With doctors and nurses looking over her, she came to the realization that she had been in a car accident. Their voices seemed miles away, as though she was seeing them from a long way off. She tried to move, but her legs were not obeying. Before the nurses could push her back down on the gurney, she leaned down to touch her legs.

"Oh, God, no!" she cried.

Her legs were warm to the touch, but they would not move. She was forced to lay down, with heavy hands on her shoulder. She kept trying to raise her knees up, but they would not budge.

"I can't feel my legs," she said in a panic to the nurse who was holding her down. "What's wrong? Why can't I feel them?"

One of the attending doctors stepped to the side of her gurney and compassionately put his hand on her shoulder, as the nurse moved away.

"We're going to run some tests to find out what's happened. It appears you have suffered a spinal injury. We'll soon have results. For now, I'm going to order a sedative to help you relax. Hopefully, we will have good news in a short while."

******

As soon as a call from the ER was made to the mansion, Sarah took down the information and immediately left a message on Charles' phone.

He was in the last song of his final performance when the message reached his phone back in the dressing room. It wasn't until he was backstage, getting ready to leave the theater and say goodbye to the conductor, that he looked into his phone and saw he had a message from Sarah. In shock, he read the message: *Abigail has been in a car accident. I don't know much. Call me for more detail. Sarah.*

He boarded the limousine and quickly made a call to Sarah.

"What happened?" he asked with terror in his voice. "Where is she, and how bad is she hurt?"

Sarah told him everything she knew, which was very little.

"She is in Waterbury," she said to Charles, choking back tears.

"What hospital?" he questioned loudly.

"Waterbury General Hospital," she said, her voice quivering. "They are running tests on her."

"I'll get my flight changed and fly into Waterbury," he said. "Call me if you hear anything more. In the meantime, I will get in touch with the ER at Waterbury to get more information."

Frantic to get a faster flight out of Sydney, he called the airline. If he had to, he would charter a plane.

There were no airline flights going into Waterbury and no charter planes available. His best bet was to board his original flight into New York. He called Marco and Ellie and then Abigail's parents.

"As soon as I know anything, I will call you," Charles assured them all.

The fight to New York City was an agonizing, twenty-five-hour flight, with one stopover. A feeling of hopelessness was gripping him, until he could hardly manage to focus on anything but reaching Abigail and the doctors. He could do nothing until he got there—nothing but pray.

Frantically, he kept calling the ER at Waterbury, asking for information and requesting that a doctor call him. He explained that he was flying home from Australia, and it would be hours before he could get there.

"Please, give my cell number to a doctor that can inform me about my wife," he pleaded with an ER associate.

Meanwhile, doctors at the hospital were going through all the tests needed to determine the extent of Abigail's injury. She had bruises and bumps that were of no immediate concern, but the preliminary tests on her spine were producing great alarm. She was conscious and talking, giving the doctors the answers they needed when pricking her legs and feet with a needle. In a short time, they would have the results of an MRI.

Six hours into the flight home, Dr. Julian Lauden, a neurosurgeon, reached Charles.

"Mr. Ricci, your wife's injury is serious," the doctor began. "We have not discussed any of it with her, as we feel you should be here when her prognosis is conferred. The images on the MRI show that her spine in the lumbar area has been severely traumatized. Images show a break at the L-4. I'm deeply sorry."

"Are you telling me that she will never walk again?" Charles said, as though the words were so dreadful, he could hardly utter them.

"I'm afraid so," the doctor concluded.

Charles was horribly shocked. He could not steady his hands. His heart started racing. He held the phone to his ear long enough to thank the doctor and tell him he would be there in a few hours. Then he dropped the phone in his lap and put his hands over his face to muffle his sobs. At that point, he didn't care who heard him, but thankfully, no one was in the seat next to him.

The word *paraplegic* saturated his mind. He could not believe that his beautiful wife would spend the rest of her life in a wheelchair. She was too young and talented for something like this to happen. Anger began to flood his emotions. He felt no urge to say a word to God. Where was He, anyway? Why did this happen? He composed himself, but inwardly, he was throwing a righteous tantrum.

His question continued to be *why?* Maybe God wanted to answer back, *why not,* which would seem heartless. Easier to not even listen for His answer.

In a peculiar sense, it seemed good that he had time before he saw Abigail to bring himself into a manageable state of control so he could help her. He looked out the oval window of the plane and felt as though he was lost in a nightmare and floating in space. *What will I say to her?*

And then, as if he couldn't avoid God any longer, he said, "What do You want me to say to Abigail and to our family? What do I say to the world?"

It seemed the response to this tragedy was that he should be thankful she was alive, not focus on the tragedy. Somehow, there had to be a purpose in this. That was his thought when thinking from a spiritual viewpoint. God promises that "all things work together for good to [those] who love [Him]." The question was *when?* Would good come with healing and restoration, or would it come in final death?

******

When Marco settled down enough to think after he had heard the tragic news, he knew his son would need him. There was nothing that could hold him back. He called Charles' cell phone and talked again with him.

"Charles, I'll meet you in New York and have the company plane there, waiting to fly us to Waterbury."

"Dad, that's perfect! I never thought of that. I'll keep you posted as we near New York."

Marco then called his airline captain and told him to have the plane ready, after explaining the situation to him.

"I want to be at LaGuardia, ready to take off as soon as Charles lands and disembarks from the commercial flight bringing him in from Sydney," he told him.

******

Charles settled back into his seat and called Abigail's parents. He knew he would drive them into a panic.

"I've got bad news," he started out saying to Abigail's mother. Is Rod there with you?"

"Yes, he's here," Irene answered.

"Okay, put the phone on speaker."

"What is it, Charles?" she asked in alarm. With the phone on speaker so both could hear, Charles broke the heartbreaking news. Irene began to cry, and Rod immediately said, "We will get a flight to Waterbury and be there as soon as we can."

******

The scene at the hospital was like every picture of tragedy. There was crying, embraces, and anxious quiet while they listened to a doctor deliver the reports of the texts. Charles held Abigail's hand, squeezing it as though to say to her, *I'm here with you, we will fight this together.*

Marco, Ellie, and Abigail's parents were there, all of them holding back their emotions and putting on a brave front as they stood in the room, listening to the doctor's report.

The doctor held nothing back. "Abigail's spine was severely traumatized, and the spinal injury she sustained has left her legs without feeling and strength. In time, she might be able to stand with props, but she will never walk. I'm deeply sorry, but this is the situation. The seatbelt held her in the seat, and she has some painful bruising. We will keep her comfortable while the bruising heals. She will need close observation and more tests in the next several days. I'll be on the floor for a couple more hours if you have further questions."

After saying that, he shook their hands and left the room.

The family gathered around Abigail and each spoke words of comfort and faith. Charles tenderly wiped the tears that were streaming down the sides of Abigail's beautiful face. What more could they say? It would be the sufficiency of God's grace that would get Abigail through this, and comfort all their hearts. What they had at this moment was the grace to be thankful she had not lost her life.

Charles insisted that the family go back home. He and Abigail needed time to be alone. Everyone could visit them after they returned to Greenwich and got situated with all that was needed to help Abigail's life be as doable as possible.

Charles left her room only when the nurses came to do something for her. Much of the time, she slept or was drowsy from sedatives that eased the pain of her bruised upper torso. When she was awake and comfortable, they talked and cried.

Most often, it's someone else's life that gets turned upside down. Shock and heartbreak belongs to others. But tragedy came to Abigail without warning. The whole gambit of loss and heartbreak was hers. She owned it, and Charles along with her. For better or worse, they found themselves on new and unfamiliar ground. They were the ones whom people would be watching on the news and reading about. Their fans would read the stories of their accident with pity, and they would wonder if she would ever perform again.

No one could tell them to accept this tragedy and move on. They were not ready for that. Abigail might never yield. No one would dare suggest they should think and feel in a different way. Not when they were riding a fearful and emotional roller coaster that had no end to it. If acceptance came to Abigail, it would take time. She would go through all the stages of grief. One moment, she would be silent; the next, she would be exhibiting all sorts of emotions. Time, lots of time, was needed to reconcile the fact that in a split second, her life was changed, and no one could click to another channel or turn off the tragedy. Life goes on in its own terms, no matter how smart or how talented a person is.

Abigail would have to surrender, or she would keep wrestling and resisting forever. Charley would be called upon time and again to show patience. He would be the empathy she needed, even if she hatefully pushed him away. He would learn through frustration and hurt to give her the right to express her anger and sorrow. Maybe in time, her spirit would heal. But for now, her life was broken, just like her spine. Her dreams and her career were shattered into a million pieces. If there was a journey back, it would be difficult to travel. It would require one step at a time, one breath at a time.

Charles watched her as she slept and recognized that her slumber was the only escape she had from the horror of her situation. He watched the panic and fear return to her when she awoke. She often awoke and would say, "Oh, Charles, I'm so glad that you're here. I thought you had left me."

He watched her reach for her legs, hoping to feel her fingers touching them. He hurt when she didn't want to hear his loving encouragement. He could never know the agony she felt, though he imagined it had to be terrible. He wanted her to realize she was still the same beautiful, smart, and talented woman she always was. If nothing else, he wanted her to feel safe that he would always be there and help her fight back. Maybe through this tragedy, both of them would become better people.

The discharge from the hospital meant they were on their own. Most people are happy to leave the sterile rooms of a medical infirmary, but when the nurse wheeled Abigail through the hospital doors and to the car, Charles felt a tremendous weight of responsibility heaped upon his shoulders. He was now the caregiver. He had sole charge of her life. Choking with responsibility, he would take on this fight with all his strength. He loved her enough that he would jeopardize his career to help her gain back her life, if it came to that.

******

The long ride from Waterbury to Greenwich was solemn. Charles spoke very little, hoping she would talk, but she remained silent. If he could get inside her thoughts, he would find that she was afraid and questioning who she was. When she left Greenwich to be at the cottage when he returned from Sydney, she could walk. Three weeks later, she was returning in a wheelchair. What could she talk about? Everything was strange and insensitive.

She felt envious, watching him sit behind the steering wheel, driving. *Look at him, so strong and handsome,* she said begrudgingly to herself. He could feel his legs. His foot could hit the brakes in a second's notice. He could walk. She had none of that. Stopping at a rest area was awkward and embarrassing. They were trained at the hospital how to handle her needs, including managing public restrooms, but the first time with him was difficult.

******

Back in Greenwich, Sarah planned carefully for their arrival, including preparing a delicious dinner. But what she had not planned for was the initial shock of seeing Abigail brought through the front door in a wheelchair. When Abbie had left weeks ago, she was a happy girl, vigorously packing the car and waving goodbye, as she rode off to the cottage. Today, she was returning as an invalid.

Sarah watched from the music room windows as Charles got the wheelchair out of the trunk and then helped Abigail get into it. It was a pathetic sight. Beautiful Abigail being helped into a wheelchair. Sarah went numb with remorse. But what saved the moment for her was when Abigail caught sight of her. While Charles wheeled her through the door, Abbie burst into tears and held her arms out for an embrace.

Human nature is hard to explain. Of all those who surrounded Abigail during the aftermath of the accident, including her own parents, Sarah would be the last person thought of to have experienced this spontaneous outburst of affection.

******

Charles stood in awe of what was taking place. He knew they shared a valuable relationship, but he was stunned to see the show of warm affection that was transpiring between them. Watching this and seeing Sarah take over the situation like a mother was a phenomenal surprise.

He looked at the two of them, wiping tears and loving each other, and said in his heart, *Now I have help.*

Chapter 9

Day and night, Abigail was being helped in and out of bed. If she dropped something, she couldn't pick it up for fear she would fall out of the wheelchair. The clothes hanging in her closet were too high for her to reach. She was frustrated when she could not reach things on the counters. If she went somewhere, she had to be helped into the car and out of the car. Life was one difficult task, and the result of her helplessness was causing great emotional stress. She was riding a rollercoaster of emotions. Anger, sadness, fear, and worry were constantly tormenting her. She was not handling her situation well. She was rebelling.

The medical staff at the hospital in Waterbury gave them helpful pamphlets to read that suggested changing many things in the house to make access better. Charles and Abigail attended a couple of classes before coming home that showed how a paraplegic's life can become independent. They were told that hiring a skilled therapist to work with her would be profitable. She could learn to fend for herself in most things, if she gained the strength and the know-how. It seemed he was riding the rollercoaster, too.

Charles got busy seeking workers to change things for easy reach, starting with the rods in her closet and building accessible drawers in their bedroom. A new walk-in shower with a built-in bench and a flush threshold was being built in the master bathroom, replacing the old one. Things were busy and noisy. Changes were being implemented as fast as Charles could get them contracted. He was also looking for a skilled therapist to hire full-time to teach Abigail to become more independent. They gave two interviews, but neither therapist suited Abigail.

In the meantime, Sarah had taken over much of the menial tasks and errands to get Abigail up and around every day. She was a genius about knowing exactly what to say and do. She discreetly got her doing small things that would make her feel productive. In the process, the hope was to help Abigail accept her condition. It seemed like Sarah's strategy was working whenever she managed to get a smile from Abigail.

As for Charles, he was learning how to treat Abigail, but it was never right. He tried not to get overly helpful to the point that made her feel helpless. He never pushed gestures of affection unless he saw she wanted to be kissed or held, and that was rare. He waited for her to give the cues about everything, and it was driving him crazy. He knew it would be a while before things between them would be like they were—and he was truly trying to be patient—but some days, he was pushed to his limit.

He stopped inviting her to listen to his practice times at the piano because she made excuses not to go into the music room. Her refusals hurt him deeply. It seemed to him that when she lost the use of her legs, she deliberately wanted to lose her love for music and singing, maybe even for him. She never talked about her career, even when bookings were offered to her. She stayed silent and cold. He would do anything in the world for her, if only she would talk with him and tell him what she was feeling. He could not help her if she wouldn't talk.

He pulled Sarah aside one day and asked her if she was comfortable to be alone with Abigail if he went to New York for a couple of days. He desperately needed the counsel of his father and Aunt Ellie. She assured him they would be fine, and without saying too much, she let him know that the struggle between him and Abigail was obvious.

"You go and spend some time with your family, Mr. Ricci," she said. "We will be just fine. I know your folks are good people, and you need them. I can call you if we run into any problems."

He would have to come up with an excuse to go. He couldn't just flat out leave.

He walked out into the terrace garden to get privacy and called Marco.

"Hi, Dad, how're things going?" he asked, as though everything was great and life was a bowl of cherries on his end.

"Things are good, Charles. How about on your end? Is Abigail doing any better?"

Charles felt himself choking. The sound of his father's voice was comforting. He felt like spilling everything out and going into a pity party, but he held back.

"Well, things are not good. Abigail is in a deep depression. I'm trying to get a skilled therapist for her because I know if she can get strong enough to do most things for herself, she will start coming around better. She sees a psychiatrist every week, but I think her problem is deeper than what a psychiatrist can help."

He paused and waited for Marco to respond.

"Would the two of you like to come to the penthouse for a few days?" Marco asked. "It's been a couple of weeks since we were with you and Abigail."

Abigail had visits and phone calls from her parents and some of her theater colleagues, but no one could bring the joy and spark back into her no matter what they said. It was as though Abigail had put a wall up that no one could get through or climb over.

"No, not the two of us. Just me. I need to talk to you and Aunt Ellie. I need to be with you for a day or two. I need some advice."

"Charles, I didn't know things were that bad. I knew it would be a struggle for Abigail to get to the point of accepting what happened, but I thought the two of you were doing well with all the problems and that they would get worked out. You get your things together and come as soon as you can."

Charles was relieved, but he needed an excuse to tell Abigail why he was going to the penthouse.

"What should I tell her, Dad? I need a valid excuse to be coming. I don't want to lie."

Marco thought for a moment and then came up with something legitimate. "I've been meaning for you to look over some things in the business trust—things that apply to you and to Anthony and Joe. It's just trivial things, but a good enough excuse for you to come."

"That sounds perfect, Dad. I'll come tomorrow morning if you have some time, and I'll stay through the next day if I need to. I've already talked to Sarah, and she's fine about being alone with Abigail for a couple of days. Unless Abigail puts up a big fuss, I'll be there in the morning."

"Call me when you're on your way tomorrow," Marco said, and they hung up.

Charles started looking for the right moment to tell Abigail that his father wanted to see him about some changes he made in the business trust. Telling her that he had to make a trip to New York should be a simple thing, but he was nervous. He never knew what to expect from her. This was his life now; he was nervous about everything he was saying and doing.

He went into the music room, sat at the piano, and played a couple of pop songs, just to stall. He was having trouble accepting what was happening to him, as well as to Abigail. He was rebelling, too. Would he and Abigail end up divorcing? Her accident should not be driving them apart. If anything needed to change, it should be that they would be closer than before. He stopped playing and walked into the kitchen.

Sarah and Abigail were busy putting a salad together for dinner. It was a perfect time to say what he needed to say, in front of Sarah. He managed to get it out matter-of-factly that he was going to New York to settle some things with his father regarding the business trust.

"It shouldn't take long. I'll leave early tomorrow morning and be back by evening the next day. Will you be okay staying here with Sarah?" he asked.

"I'll be fine; you go," Abigail said rather abruptly.

"Great," he said and looked at Sarah.

Abigail kept her head down, looking into the bowl of lettuce resting in her lap, as she continued to tear the lettuce into small pieces. Sarah looked at Charles and winked at him. It was done, and he was feeling some relief.

Abigail was very quiet when they went to bed. He helped her out of the wheelchair after she brushed her teeth and put on a nightgown. He loved picking her up and putting her into bed. It was the only time he was physically close to her. She was rigid and rarely allowed him to move close to her. And he was wanting desperately to tell her that he loved her more than ever and wanted so much to be close to her. He was afraid she didn't love him because he was strong and able. He imagined it was jealousy that might be keeping her from him, jealous that she was impaired and he was strong and healthy. He felt guilty.

******

It was strange, the two of them sharing the bed and both of them drawing an invisible line between them. She was afraid, but she loved him and needed him more than ever. But she couldn't bring herself to tell him. She felt that she was not beautiful anymore; the accident had changed everything. The situation seemed so deeply impossible that the two of them could not share their deepest thoughts and feelings.

******

Ellie had warm cinnamon rolls baking in the oven and fresh coffee brewing when Charles arrived at the penthouse. It felt like old times to him, the three of them sitting at the breakfast table, talking. At first, they chatted about general things, and then Marco went into the business of the trust, which was something trivial and took no time at all. Not even a signature was needed.

Ellie suggested they move out onto the terrace.

"Take your coffee with you," she said, picking up the empty plates and putting them into the sink.

Charles loved the view of tall buildings from the terrace and never got tired of hearing the sound of traffic. Being home with Aunt Ellie and his father created a momentary feeling like everything was good again. But it wasn't, and he didn't know where to begin discussing what his life with Abigail had become.

"So, Charles, how's it going with you and Abigail?" Marco said, opening up the conversation.

"Not good, Dad."

He set his coffee mug down and tried to relax into the rattan chair.

"I love Abigail more than anything, and I'll do anything in the world for her, but she is keeping me out. She won't talk. She's cold and unloving. I know she is mourning over the loss of her legs and the fact that she is crippled for life. It's got to be terrible, but she won't let me in. I can't help her if she won't let me."

He swallowed the lump in his throat. Those were the only words he knew to explain how things were going. He was there with the only two people in all the world who would understand. Their unconditional love gave him a sense of safety and belonging. Nothing needed to be changed or hidden. Their love for him was solid, without any conditions attached and regardless of flaws or mistakes.

Marco sat there, stunned that things had become so difficult.

Ellie had plenty to say.

"Well, she's dealing with the first stage of her injury, the physical part. She is focusing on never walking again. She's probably thinking that she's to blame, or maybe God is punishing her. She probably thinks she's ugly, too."

There was no stopping Ellie when she got started on something. Most of the time, she was right.

"She is going to build a new life for herself, regardless of the fact that she is married to you. The intimate and psychological problems that she has suffered from this accident are hers to deal with, regardless of how much you love her and help her. It's all baked into the cake, so to speak. It's frightening to her. She sees herself as worthless now. Until she is able to accept the challenge to move forward, she will rebel against every suggestion to help her. Rebellion is a way of coping. That sounds strange, but it is an emotional mechanism."

Charles listened and knew that what Ellie was saying made sense. The therapists at the hospital said much of the same to him. The pamphlets they came home with communicated the same things. Before Abigail could move on, she would need to admit that the accident happened without regard to good or bad. She had to believe that God still had a plan for her life. Her life was definitely going to proceed in a wheelchair. How it proceeded was up to her.

"Aunt Ellie, I know you are right," Charles said. "It's up to Abigail to want to move forward. We've been warned that it takes time. It won't happen all of a sudden. She will have good days and bad days. The depression will be like a vicious dog coming after her. The fear she has about losing her independence is like suffocating for air, even though she is still breathing."

Ellie picked up from there. "Absolutely right, Charles, and you will often need to exhibit tough love and force her to react appropriately when she starts acting impossible."

They talked for a long time. One thing was sure in their conversations—that serious knowledge and understanding about paraplegia was needed. If returning back home was anything like "the beginning of wisdom" from God, Charles would need plenty of it. He would need wise insight into Abigail's ever-changing feelings. Compassion and common sense would need to lead every decision.

He would need to learn when to give in and when to hold back. His part in this crisis was as heavy as Abigail's.

That evening, they had dinner at Sardi's in Midtown Manhattan. Like old times, they saw people they knew and chatted with a couple of friends eating at the next table. It was good being there, but not so good for Charles without Abigail. He was putting on a good front. Anyone who looked at him would never guess how hurt he was. They would never know that tragedy had suddenly hit him. They had no idea that the love of his life was sitting in a wheelchair in Greenwich, Connecticut, and that he wanted desperately to be there with her and make things better.

After dinner, they walked several blocks, talking and reminiscing before hailing a cab and returning to the penthouse. New York had not changed, but Charles had. A few people recognized him, and he politely spoke, but everything felt flat and meaningless.

Back at the penthouse, before they went to bed, Marco gathered Ellie and Charles into the great room for prayer. He didn't feel that he should ask for a miracle. God would have given that at the accident. The thing Charles and Abigail needed most was to know that God was in control of their situation and had their futures safe in His hand. That was his prayer.

Saying goodnight to each other was emotional. The comfort of family and prayers was reassuring, but Charles was still full of anxiety. He told them he would not be spending tomorrow in New York but would leave for Greenwich after breakfast. He knew he needed to get back home, even though it meant facing Abigail and her rebellion again.

He slept in the same bedroom he had before moving to Greenwich, but it seemed cold, almost morbid this night. It wasn't warm and inviting. It felt strange, like a forecast being read to him that his life would never be happy again. He was in this room just weeks ago with Abigail, after enjoying a great time at a party in honor of the healing he had received in his right hand. Tonight, there was no party, no music, and no laughter, just sadness. The healing of his hand seemed trivial to what Abigail needed. An irrational thought flashed through his mind; maybe God would heal Abigail. Maybe He would put her spine back together. He knew God could do anything, but he also knew that he would hurt himself more if he began thinking that Abigail was going to walk again. The doctor's words and the image reports were firm. She would never walk again.

He remembered that the apostle Paul in the Bible had a major problem that was of great concern. This apostle called it "a thorn in the flesh." He begged God three times to take it away, but it remained. Instead of healing, he was told that God's grace would be sufficient for him to bear it. He was assured that in his weakness, he would receive strength to bear it. This was the answer for Abigail. God would give her strength to bear the loss of her legs. In this weakness, she would become strong. Her life was still valuable and promising. Oh, if she would only believe that!

He called her before turning off the lights.

"Hi, sweetheart, are you getting ready for bed?" he asked her.

"I'm already in bed reading," she answered.

"Oh, well, how did your day go?" he inquired.

"It was fine. I asked Sarah to join me for lunch in the terrace garden. I hope you don't mind that I did that. You know, her being a domestic employee and all."

"Why would I mind?" he asked, thinking that Abigail did that because she didn't want to eat. "I think part of her job now is to do things for you, and if eating lunch together is what you want, you should do it."

It was loneliness that Abigail was feeling and deep enough that she required Sarah to eat with her. But the truth was that Charles was as lonely as Abigail.

There was a pause in their conversation. Charles waited for her to continue talking, but she stayed silent. The entire phone call seemed awkward. It was nothing like the calls he had made from Sydney, when the sound of their voices made them happy and lonesome for each other.

"I'll be home tomorrow morning," he said, breaking the silence. "Dad went over the business trust with me today, and there is no reason for me to stay tomorrow."

"Okay," she said, and that was it. The conversation ended with him saying goodnight.

He would be better off to go home and not look for any quick changes in her attitude, even considering the prayer that was just prayed by Marco. She was hanging on tight to her pitiful state of morbidity. He put the phone down and turned off the light.

Diving home early the next morning, he thought of the things he still had to do to get Abigail the help she needed. The first on his agenda was to keep looking for a physical therapist. The next was to buy a van with a hydraulic lift to get Abigail and the wheelchair up and down from the vehicle. In time, he would look into getting her behind the wheel and driving again. He was sure there was a hand instrument that would operate the brake.

Once he reached Greenwich, he stopped and bought a bouquet of roses. It just seemed like something was telling him to do that. Next, he stopped at the candy store and bought a bag of chocolate pecan clusters that he knew she loved.

He found her in the terrace garden when he arrived. She looked as beautiful as ever, sitting there in the shade of the trees, looking into the thick, wooded brush beyond their property. She was wearing a blue, silk shirt, rolled up to her elbows. White jeans ran smoothly down her legs and hit just above her brown, leather sandals. Her hair fell soft upon her shoulders. She heard his footsteps and turned toward him.

He walked up and handed the roses to her.

"These roses aren't half as beautiful as you are. I stopped at the candy store and got you some of those chocolate pecan clusters you love so much."

She took the roses, and then he handed her the bag of chocolates.

She started to cry. It was like something gave way all of a sudden, and she simply let it go. Her cry broke into a sob, as she buried her head into the bouquet of roses.

He knelt down at her wheelchair and took her hands into his hands and began kissing them, as if he wasn't sure what to do next.

"It's just that you're being so tender to me, and it's more wonderful than I can bear," she sobbed.

He gathered her into his arms and said, "Abbie, I love you more than anything in this world."

His words seemed to fill the terrace garden with music. He buried his head in her lap, roses and all, and cried as if it didn't matter that he was a man.

Everything that was bottled up in both of them was finding its way out.

She stroked his hair and said, "Charlie, I love you, too. I can't live without you."

Still kneeling, he took her into his arms and tenderly kissed her.

"I missed you so much when you were gone," she said to him. "I felt like my life left with you when you drove off to New York. I knew if you didn't come back, I would die."

"Abbie, I'll always be here for you. I love you too much to ever leave." He stood up. "Do you want to go back into the house?"

"No, let's just stay here and talk. I have so much I want to say."

Something wonderful took place that morning. It was as if they realized how deep their love was for each other. Their lost intimacy and compassion for each other emerged fresh and new. They took the God-inspired invitation to find each other again.

Chapter 10

As Providence does often intercede in difficult situations, a physical therapist by the name of Meg contacted Abigail. In step with every event in Abigail's life since she had met Charles, unexplained and unsolved things were beginning to find some light. This surprise contact appeared to be God-arranged. Meg happened to hear from a colleague that Abigail was looking for a therapist during the time she was finishing up with another patient. She had the outstanding credentials and professional character that could nail the contract with Abigail, and sure enough, she started the next day.

Meg was a harsh, down-to-business therapist. There was nothing easy about her. And that was okay because Abigail was ready to grit her teeth and bear whatever it would take to increase her arm strength and get her independently maneuvering.

Meg was ten years older than Abigail, and the difference in their age gave her an edge. She could demand and push without appearing like a young twerp trying to show off. She was like an army sergeant, spewing orders and demanding they be carried out. Tears never coaxed her to let up. In fact, she was acquainted with tears because she knew they were part of the process. But with her harshness also came compassion. If Abigail became too stressed, she would back off.

The schedule called for her to work four days a week, arriving in the morning while Abigail was fresh and ready for a workout. It was all work and no play, until one day Abigail was tired. She asked Meg to join her in a cup of tea at the breakfast table. It just happened that Meg was running late that morning and had left her house without breakfast, so the tea sounded good.

"Would you like a toasted bagel?" she asked Meg, thinking she might be hungry.

"Oh, that would be great. I rushed out without breakfast this morning," she said, while stirring sugar into her tea.

For a short moment, Abigail became the center of attention, getting the bagels out of the pantry, setting up the toaster, and putting butter and jelly on the table. She was showing off to Meg that she could get around the kitchen quickly in the wheelchair.

"See how efficient I am in the kitchen," she said cheerfully, getting a knife out of the cutlery drawer and setting it at Meg's place.

Maneuvering from counter to counter quickly and reaching for things in the cabinets were just some of the accomplishments she was making since Meg had started working with her. The first triumph was mastering everything in her bedroom; getting in and out of bed without help was a major feat. Transferring onto the shower chair from the wheelchair without Charles' help was another achievement. It took strength to do these things; and to gain that amount of strength meant she must do vigorous calisthenics every day.

Abigail was happy for the break in today's therapy session and even more pleased that Meg was taking time to have a quick breakfast. She had grown to like her as a friend. "Tell me about yourself, Meg. I don't know much about you," she inquired.

"There's not much to tell. I'm divorced, and I don't have any children," she responded, rather matter-of-factly.

"Oh, I'm sorry you are divorced. How long have you been single?" Abigail asked, sincerely wanting to know more about her.

"Five years," she said. "We were married just one year and renting an apartment. I had no professional skills at the time and was left with nothing after the divorce. At the time, I was working as a receptionist in a doctor's office and needed a better paying job."

She stopped and sipped her tea and then went on.

"I really enjoyed interfacing with the patients when they came in and registered at my desk. It seemed fitting to pursue something in the medical field. I decided to get a degree in physical therapy. I love this work, especially with patients who are paraplegic."

Abigail was truly impressed.

"Looking at what you are accomplishing with me, I can say with authority that you went into the right profession. I couldn't get out of bed without help before you came. I was also very depressed, and that has been greatly helped," Abigail said.

Meg shook her head in agreement.

"You are doing extremely well. Actually, you are one of the best patients I've worked with."

"It's all you and the good Lord," Abigail responded. "I couldn't do this without both of you."

Meg put her tea cup back in the saucer, and without hesitating, she said with excitement, "You're a Christian!"

Abigail shook her head yes.

"I am, too! No wonder we work so well together."

She laughed and went on talking.

"You know, I could tell that you and your husband were different, and I wondered if you were Christians. But who goes around asking that question? I don't."

"Well, this is really funny," Abigail said. "I thought the same about you, but I didn't want to come right out and ask."

And there it was again, Providence working and providing exactly what was needed. This conversation would never have taken place if it were not for Sarah being at the grocery store and Charles at Natalie's office going over his performance schedule. When life slows down for a few minutes, good things can happen.

"Well, come on," Meg said, "we have work to do. Today, let's tackle the music room, but how about not until you run through a few of your calisthenics."

The music room was still a difficult room for Abigail. She could sit at the piano with Charles on occasion, but she shied away from singing when he played and always refused to engage in conversations about her career. Charles patiently backed off when he saw she didn't want to talk about it. Once in a while, he could get her to sing with him, but she would not sing just *for* him alone. Even more heartbreaking were the invitations to perform laying in the desk tray, unanswered. Her fan club blog indicated that she was greatly missed, but her struggle about the future continued.

She wheeled into the music room behind Meg, dreading to get into all the stuff that would be discussed about where her files and music were located and if her video cabinet was functional. She knew Meg would ask her about the piano and if she played and if it was difficult for her to sit on the bench. It was like opening up a can of worms and then being put through the third degree.

Meg stood in the middle of the room, hands on her hips, admiring the view of the front lawn.

"How far is it to the beach?" she asked.

"Not far, less than a quarter of a mile," Abigail responded.

"Have you ever gone down there on your own?" Meg pried.

"Absolutely not!" Abigail's forceful answer should have stopped the beach talk right there, but it didn't.

"Well, would you like to go down there?" Meg asked, as if she had found another area to open up for Abigail.

"I don't know. I never thought about it. There is solid sidewalk all the way down to where we like to go. But Charles has never asked if he could wheel me down there. I think that area is off-limits."

"Okay, once we get you completely functional here in the house, we will tackle that. You never know; someday, you may want to venture to the beach on your own.

"You sound like you're getting me ready to live by myself someday," Abigail said sadly.

"That's exactly why I'm here. You need to become independent if that day ever comes."

Meg took a good look around the room and started asking where things were stored and what files Abigail would be getting into. They worked steadily, making some changes for convenience, and then stopped at the video cabinet.

"Wow, you certainly have a lot of DVDs," Meg said, opening up the cabinet. "A lot of them you cannot reach. Are there some that should be stored farther down?"

"Oh, Meg, we don't need to get into those videos," Abigail pleaded. "They're films of my performances. Some are Charles', too. Let's just leave them alone for now."

The last thing she wanted was to have a conversation about her career. But she knew Meg was aware of her career and that she was fighting talking about her future.

Meg took out a DVD of Abigail performing at Carnegie Hall.

"I would love to see this," she said, glancing over at the television set at the other end of the music room.

"No, please! I'd rather not," Abigail said, in a tone that was pleading.

Meg knew that Abigail was allowing her fear to hold her hostage. Her fear of how it would affect her fans to see her performing in a wheelchair was crawling all over her like a suffocating octopus. Of all the places Abigail wanted complete independence, Meg knew it was on stage. But she also knew that this anxiety over the wheelchair could be conquered if Abigail would concentrate on who she was, rather than the wheelchair. The wheelchair did not define Abigail, but she was allowing it to have predominance.

Meg smartly countered back, "I've heard what a beautiful voice you have. I'd love to watch this. Couldn't we just see a little of it?"

"It only has one song on it, and it's not that good," Abigail said, hoping that Meg would let up. She didn't want to be rude to her, but she wasn't ready to look at any of her videos and see herself standing at a piano or in front of a floor microphone. She just couldn't bear to see how she once was.

"One song is plenty; that's all I want to watch," Meg said. And before Abigail could say any more, she switched to another conversation, which was the speech she gave to all paraplegics when she suspects there might be a little hope of them getting out of the wheelchair.

"I've seen your medical reports," she began. "I had to study them in order to know how to work with you and understand the type of injury you have. You won't walk, that's for sure, but there's nothing to hold you back from trying to stand if you're propped up. I had one patient who had an injury similar to yours. We worked on his upper torso muscles to get them strong enough to help him balance and stand with braces on his legs. He could stand by leaning against something solid. He couldn't stand for a long length of time, but long enough to give a speech."

She paused for a moment seeing that Abigail looked bothered. But the army sergeant in her was revved up to high pitch, and she kept talking.

"I am not saying that this is possible for you, but I am saying that it would be something to look into."

This was absurd to think that she would ever be able to stand without someone helping her. Whoever that man was, his case had to be completely different than hers. Abigail could feel herself bristling, as though Meg might be exploiting her situation. But yet, the idea had touched a place in her mind that yearned to know. If ever there was a possibility of something more than the wheelchair, she wanted it.

She had never asked God for a miracle. That would be like asking for a baby without a womb. She just wanted to have something beyond the wheelchair.

It was uncanny how this conversation came out of the blue, and if there was any value to it, it was the nudge to look at the DVD that Meg was holding in her hand.

"Meg, I really do not want to pursue leg braces and hard, vigorous exercise to see if I can stand. I've come to grips with the truth that what the doctors saw in the MRI told the story that I will never walk, and I know I will never stand. But believe me, you touched me with your excited interest. Ever since you started working with me, I feel as though there is something waiting for me. I don't know what it is, but there is something out there for me. Go ahead, play the DVD. I'll cry, so you better get ready for that."

This was exactly what Meg wanted to hear from Abigail, that the progress she was making with the physical therapy was helping her consider her future. Abigail already had that *special something* waiting for her—it was her voice, the gift of singing and inspiring people. How it was going to work out, only she and the Lord knew.

Meg started the DVD and then sat down. Abigail wheeled over by her, nervous and anxious. The show started. The camera was on the orchestra at first and then panned over to Abigail. She was standing in front of a floor mic in a beautiful aqua, floor-length gown that softly hugged her slim body.

"Beautiful!" Meg said. "You're absolutely beautiful—and still are."

The song was "Over the Rainbow." Was Providence still working? The words seemed to catch what they were discussing. It was like a storybook tale of hope.

Somewhere skies are blue. The storms are over. Somewhere dreams really do come true. If happy bluebirds fly, then why couldn't Abigail fly to whatever it was her future held?

The whole thing with Meg pushing her was just too much. Abigail started to cry; and the army sergeant personality backed down in Meg. It was just too much for both of them.

Sarah came back from the grocery store and walked into the music room to let Abigail know she was back home and the groceries were all put away.

"What's wrong?" she asked, thinking that another tragedy had happened when she saw Abigail crying.

"We're okay," Meg said. "We just watched one of Abigail's DVDs.

Sarah was shocked.

"Abigail wouldn't have anything to do with those DVDs or even talk about singing," she said to Meg. Then she looked at Abigail and asked, "Are you okay?"

Before Abigail could answer Charles was back home, and he walked into the music room to see what was going on.

"What in the world is happening?" he asked, noticing Abigail wiping her eyes.

"Nothing," Sarah piped up, sort of crying, too. "Your wife just watched one of her DVDs."

******

Charles was stunned. His first thought was that Meg was messing with something she had no business doing. He was starting to get angry, thinking that Abigail was upset.

"I don't think that was a good idea to have Abbie watching one of her DVDs," he said crossly.

"Charlie, I'm fine," Abigail explained. "I told Meg to do that. I think I needed to watch that DVD. It was the performance at Carnegie Hall. Remember? You were there?"

He didn't say any more. What more was there to say with three ladies acting emotional? What man could deal with that? He turned around and left the room, without realizing the significance of what had taken place.

There was a lot to be said later that evening when Abigail had a chance to talk with Charles. First, he found out that Meg was a Christian. Then, she told him about the conversation she and Meg had had that led to her watching that DVD.

"Charlie, I'm telling you the truth. I started to get a whole different perspective on my situation regarding my career. I seemed to sense that there might be something for me to do that is different than what I was doing. I don't know what it is, but I believe there is something new out there. Maybe I should simply go back on stage in a wheelchair. Maybe that's what is different—the wheelchair. Maybe it will have a significant impact. What do you think?"

He had waited several months for her to get to this point of realization—that she was still a valuable woman and had something more to do. Whatever it was that she wanted to do, he would help her do it. She was too talented to keep wasting her gift. As for her emotional outburst in the music room, he understood it. He was understanding why all three of them were emotional when he came home. The impact of Abigail watching one of her performances proved that she was beginning to look positively at herself and her future. Whenever something speaks to the soul, it often brings emotion. He thought back to the roses and the bag of chocolate pecan clusters in the terrace garden. What an emotional moment that was, both of them crying and coming to their senses.

"I don't know what to think," he said. "I do know one thing; I've been waiting and hoping for this moment when you would want to get back on stage and sing again—or at least start seeking what you should be doing with your talent. We need to look at it carefully from every angle. Getting you on and off airplanes and to the theaters and then to your hotel rooms is going to take some ingenuity. Most of all, I want you to be safe."

There was plenty to think about. Theater invitations to perform were still coming in. Managers and fans were not giving up. They still wanted her. All she needed to do was accept one of the invitations, and that would automatically put her back on stage, performing whenever she desired.

"It's such a beautiful evening. The sun hasn't set yet; let's go down to the beach," he said. "We haven't looked at Long Island Sound for a long time."

******

Providence at work again? Meg had discussed the beach with her that day. She wanted to go down there. More so with him pushing the wheelchair than Meg wanting her to learn to make that trip on her own.

It was wonderful being wheeled down to the beach and breathing fresh, salty air. The sun was still well above the linden trees. They had plenty of time to reach the beach and get back before it set. The fresh air was invigorating; she felt like someone receiving their walking papers to leave a hydrophobic environment and come out of a prison cell. The sound of the waves washing on shore was like the steady rhythm of her heart, passionately moving her forward into whatever her future would hold.

******

Charles was booked for a one-night performance in Dallas. He offered to take Abigail, but she was happy to stay home, since he would be back the next day. This trip would be a good chance to observe how he would maneuver Abigail through an airport. He needed to study how he would get her on and off the plane and manage everything involved to get her back on stage. He would look at the difficulty to get to the theaters and to the hotels. The trip would be a pilot run for Abigail. The airlines would, of course, be notified that she needed special provisions, but he would use this trip to see how easy or difficult her travel might be.

On the flight home from Dallas, he was absorbed with thoughts. One thought that came to him just might work. What if a piano was rolled out on stage and he played for her? That might give her more confidence. The orchestra would be in the background, and the piano could take some of the harsh focus off of Abigail in a wheelchair. Of course, she could sing at any place on stage she desired, but if she was next to the piano, it might give her more poise. Meg was working hard to get her to stand with the support of her arm placed on a piano, or on a different prop, and the custom-made leg braces would help steady her. He couldn't wait to get home and present this idea to her.

******

"Well, what do you think? Can we try it?" he asked her. "It does not need to be advertised that Charles Ricci is playing for his wife."

She thought about it for a moment. Was this the *something different* she felt was coming to her? Was that it—that Charles would play the piano for her? Was this right for him to do? He would still have his own career, so maybe it would work. But there was no way they could keep the public from knowing he was playing the piano. People could spot Charles in a jam-packed airport.

"I like the idea," she said. "Having you on stage with me would be a great benefit, at least to begin with. If you didn't want to continue doing this, or your schedule interfered, I'm sure I could manage with someone else playing the piano. Sarah or Natalie could travel with me. I don't see how it would hurt my career one bit, having the great Charles Ricci playing piano for me."

"Okay, then, let's give it a try," Charles said. "I can arrange my performances so they do not conflict with yours."

He got up and put his arms around her, squeezed her tight, and kissed her.

"I can see it now," he said and laughed, standing in front of her as though he was an announcer holding a microphone in his hand.

"Ladies and gentlemen, it's Ricci and Ricci on stage for the first time!"

Chapter 11

It was months since Charles had written the concerto that Natalie had sent to Conductor Henry Rosenbaum in London for consideration. His intense involvement with Abigail after her accident had caused him to forget about it. At the beginning, he had hoped that Rosenbaum would like it and have it performed by a pianist, accompanied by the London Core Symphony playing in the background. Simply having it out there for an audience to hear was enough. He did not require that he be the pianist to perform it. So it was a huge surprise when word came from Rosenbaum that he liked the creative work and wanted Charles to perform it.

"Mr. Charles Ricci?" Rosenbaum inquired on the phone.

"Yes, it is," Charles responded.

"This is Henry Rosenbaum from the London Core Symphony Orchestra. I like your concerto, "The Flight of the Birds." The movements in it are crisp, and you inspire my imagination when I hear it played. My orchestra has played it several times as a practice exercise, and every musician is impressed with it. Would you consider coming to London and playing for me at a performance, or can I buy the rights to play it?"

Charles was dazed for a moment. In all the involvement of Abigail's accident, he had not thought about the concerto for months. He quickly gathered his thoughts and responded.

"Well, thank you, sir. Yes, I would like to come to London and perform my concerto with your orchestra. You'll note that I creatively wrote each musician's part of accompaniment, so the entire piece can be easily synchronized. I know it is unconventional to have more than one instrument performing a concerto, but like so many things in the twenty-first century, new works arise and often get highly accepted."

Rosenbaum quickly agreed. "Yes, and that is why I like it. I believe it is a perfect piece to present to audiences. The music world is ready for something new. Would you be able to come to London in two weeks and perform one evening at the Burne Hall? There is an opening for another performer. I'm referring to the show, *A Night to Remember*. You would fit perfectly into the program because you are the author of the piece you will perform, and it is a new work." He continued before Charles could comment. "You no doubt have read about the Burne Hall and seen photographs of it. It opened for the new season four weeks ago. Amazingly, all twenty-eight hundred seats were filled."

Indeed, Charles had read about this and saw the photos. It was an awesome theater. He never dreamed he would perform there—not until he could get farther along in his career. The performers were stars from all over the world. It was hard to believe he was being invited.

While he sat listening to Rosenbaum talk, he was bubbling with excitement.

"Oh yes, I have seen photos of the Burne Hall and read about the season opening. It's a magnificent hall. Yes, I believe I can work that into my schedule. Can we get back to each other about particulars tomorrow, after I look at my schedule? I'm sure we can firm everything up."

"Certainly," Rosenbaum said. "I will reserve four seats for you for whomever you invite. If we can do this, there will be full accommodations offered for all in your party. I'm sure we can come to a generous agreement on your fee. I'll call tomorrow."

Charles hung the phone up and simply reveled in what he had just been offered. This was like a dream come true. He raced to find Abigail and tell her.

"Abbie, we're going to London in two weeks!" he shouted, when he found her in the great room. "Rosenbaum just called and wants me to perform the concerto at the Burne Hall in London."

"Oh, my goodness!" Abigail squealed. "This is wonderful! It's what you have worked so hard to get. I've got chills just thinking about it. Do you think I can go with you without any trouble?"

"I wouldn't go without you," Charles confirmed, as though that question didn't even exist. "We both worked hard for this performance. You will go with me and sit in the audience as my prized fan."

For Charles, this moment was like a well-earned promotion. Like a violinist who humbly sits in the last seat of the string section of an orchestra and is promoted to the first seat. Or a newspaper stringer promoted to editor. The feeling of accomplishment was the same to him, no matter what a person's position is. He had written the composition when his hand was crippled and painful, but now he would play it as though he had never been hurt or discouraged.

******

Abigail stared at him in wonder, as the news of this London invitation sunk in. She also had forgotten about the concerto. But quickly she started remembering when he played it for her before her accident and how convinced she was that it was good enough for the whole world to hear. Now to hear him say, "We're going to London" made her excited, but nervous. How could she manage a trip to London?

"Oh, my goodness, Charlie, that's wonderful!" she said, continuing in their excitement. "This is what you have dreamed of." She held back her concerns about making the trip in a wheelchair.

He didn't wait for her to continue talking but grabbed her wheelchair, spun it around, and then kissed her. He was feeling on top of the world. He was acting like a kid going to Disney World.

"For sure, you're going with me!" he said firmly. "There will be no ifs or buts. We can manage this, and I'm already thinking that my dad, and Aunt Ellie, and Natalie should go with us. We can invite your parents some other time. We have four seats offered to us. What do you think?"

What a change in plans this was for Abigail. She thought the next big thing in her life would be performing on stage with Charles, not going to London. If she was honest, going to Dallas or even California would be much easier than all the way to London. She began to feel stressed, but she couldn't disappoint him. Not with all he had done for her. She needed to be in London with him, wheelchair and all.

"Well, it might be a little difficult, this being our first trip on an airplane," she said. "And sitting in the audience in a wheelchair is a new experience for me. But I could never stay home, Charlie. We will work it out."

Of course, they would work it out. Charles would see to it that the airline knew beforehand that Abigail would be boarding in a wheelchair. He would make sure that the hotel was handicap-accessible, and he would see to it that Abigail sat in the aisle of her choice. They studied the seating chart of the auditorium together and would reserve where she chose to sit.

"With my family and Natalie with us, you have nothing to worry about," Charles assured her. "You'll be well taken care of, but best of all, you will be with me the entire trip and seated in my audience."

The Burne Hall was the most beautiful hall that Charles had performed in. The seats on the main floor were set into three large sections. There were two separated inner aisles. A ten-row balcony spanned above the main floor. The auditorium colors were deep red and gold. The hall resembled something built for a king.

The hall was packed when Charles' family was ushered in. Abigail's wheelchair was placed in the aisle at Marco's left, where he seated himself in the first seat of the row. Next to him was Ellie, and then Natalie. They were five rows back from the stage, sitting in a perfect view of the stage.

Charles was slated to be the third performer of six.

The curtain went up, and the show began. Many months had passed since Abigail was in one of Charles' audiences, and the feeling she had was like coming home. The anxiety of the long ordeal she had gone through and getting to this point of travel faded away. She felt as though she was in a dream. Everything seemed surreal and wonderful. Of all the places she dreamed she would visit again, London was the last. Memories of their honeymoon flashed through her mind. In a hundred years, no one could have guessed that she would return in a wheelchair.

Charles was now next on the program. The crowd gave him a round of vigorous applause while he walked across the stage toward the piano.

******

In Marco's eyes, his son resembled a handsome, young maestro. Watching him bow in appreciation to the audience, he was overjoyed and proud. The only link missing was Charles' mother, Katie. If she was here, the circle would be complete. But then, as he glanced at Abigail and saw the joy and pride on her face, he could let the memory of Katie go. It seemed that Abigail was connecting the circle tonight. She was filling the hole in their hearts.

More wonderful than what was heard and imagined in the music room at Greenwich during those weeks when Charles wrote and played the concerto with the fingers of his left hand, the "Flight of the Birds" came alive. The audience of three thousand sat mesmerized. Rosenbaum's baton and hand movements kept the orchestra soft. Just one crescendo, played precisely where it should be, brought the audience into startled expectation of what might come next. It was no surprise that Charles' performance championed a standing ovation. "Flight of the Birds" was enthusiastically accepted by this London audience. From this moment on, the concerto would be played and recognized worldwide. Oh, how true it was that God brings good out of bad and has a plan for every life. If Charles had never injured his hand, the "Flight of the Birds" would never have been written.

******

Abigail clapped and wiped tears as the audience stood to their feet and applauded. Her tears were tears of joy for the love of her life, who made it to the top with this star performance. If he never went any further, this was far enough for her.

Her tears were also because she could not stand up on her feet for him. She felt humbled, in a sad, humiliating way. She was missing out on the excitement of the audience, who were on their feet applauding and some yelling bravo.

Beside her was Marco, on his feet standing. Ellie and Natalie were also standing, wildly clapping. This was a new experience—sitting during an ovation. The sad realization that she was left wanting was daring to take away her joy for Charles. Not being able to stand during an ovation was something she had not thought of while learning to become independent. It was another heart-wrenching thing to accept. But she pulled herself together and would not allow self-pity to spoil the moment.

Marco, sensing her situation, bent down and gave her a warm, loving hug.

"He's made it to the top tonight," he said to her. "We're so proud of him."

Indeed, he had made it to the top tonight, and Abigail clearly sensed that she needed to put the focus on Charles, not herself and her paraplegia. His title had now changed from just an accomplished and well-noted pianist to a music writer as well. Conductor Henry Rosenbaum had graciously given him the chance of a lifetime. If he never played in Vienna or Amsterdam, it didn't matter. He had reached the soul-satisfying pinnacle he desired.

Charles turned and bowed to Rosenbaum with an arm gesture toward him so the audience would applaud his superb conducting. Just as expected, the audience burst into loud clapping, and then Rosenbaum gave the gesture back to Charles. Whistles and more bravos filled the hall.

Unexpectedly, Charles motioned to a stagehand to bring him a hand mic. He had not planned this, but there was something he must say.

The audience quieted down, and everyone took their seats again. The spotlight came down on Charles as everyone waited.

"Thank you, London and world fans! It's great to be here." Applause broke out again. He went on.

"Burne Hall is a magnificent hall, and I am honored to be here. I am also honored and blessed to have my beautiful wife, Abigail, here in the audience."

Many in the audience knew she was a popular singer in the U.S. Some in the audience had attended her performances and knew about her accident.

"As many of you know, about a year ago, Abigail suffered an accident that took away the use of her legs. She has made tremendous progress, and she truly is the star tonight. She is my star! Her courage has been an inspiring gift in my life. She was the inspiration for the concerto, 'Flight of the Birds.' Thank you, darling." And he looked toward her and motioned to where she was sitting and blew a kiss to her.

A spotlight quickly searched the audience, and Marco gave the signal where she was sitting. The light centered down on her, and in a movement of love and appreciation, she gave back the gesture of blowing a kiss back to Charles.

This was a night they would remember for the rest of their lives. It was filled with unfailing love and the promise of a wonderful future. The world was wide open for them. All they needed to do was go through the doors.

Natalie took on the role of being an agent for Abigail and sought a theater for her first comeback performance. She was able to book her at the Radio City Music Hall in New York. A perfect place to begin. The entire family would be there, including her parents.

He had missed her last performance, before her accident, when she sang Kelly Clarkson's hit, "I Dare You."

"Let's put that song into your repertoire. It could become one of our signature songs," he said. "You'll have the audience begging for more."

Indeed, Charles was right. The audience and fans loved it and loved having her back, even in a wheelchair. The lyrics were perfect, having to do with daring yourself to love and to do what you want to do. New York was where her career had started, and New York was where it was picked up again.

Radio City Music Hall was just the beginning. There were other great performances, with Abigail comfortably performing in a wheelchair and sometimes standing, propped up at the side of the piano. Word got out into the media that Charles was playing for her. Speculation was that he would eventually do a few numbers of his own during a performance. They were right. Abigail insisted that he come out of the shadows and also perform. Thus, Ricci and Ricci was no longer a laughing joke between them; they were becoming a fascinating team. Automatically, or perhaps, providentially, Abigail's performances began to be booked as Ricci and Ricci, and their popularity grew more than when they were a single act.

Could this be the *something else* that Abigail felt the day she watched the DVD with Meg? Was Ricci and Ricci the team their futures were meant for? Their audiences loved them, whether they performed together or apart. But together, they might be able to have an impact on people who were hurting and searching for help. Combining as a team might make it easier to incorporate a gospel song or two in their performances. Maybe they could consider working in some inspiring dialogue. For certain, they each had a message of faith and hope to give to a hurting world. They seemed to be hearing a message that God was working out a beautiful plan for their lives, maybe better than before. Together, they were reaching the same rainbow's end, where God's will for their lives was the pot of gold.

******

Coming home from the Boston Symphony Hall, where they entertained a packed auditorium, Abigail slept most of the way. The next day, Charles thought she looked tired.

"Are you okay, Abbie?" he asked.

"Yes, I'm okay. I just feel tired a lot of the time. Maybe it's our busy schedule," she answered.

He was worried about her. She was not eating well either.

"Maybe you should see your doctor earlier than your next scheduled appointment," he suggested.

She thought he was being overly protective, but he would not stop nagging her, so she made the appointment. Charles, of course, went with her as he always did since her accident.

In the many months since her accident, she had gone through umpteen routine examinations, only to be told that she was doing fine. But this time it was not the routine answer she expected.

As normal procedure, the doctor always had Abigail and Charles come into his office afterward, and he would discuss the results of the examination and have a nice time chatting with them. They suspected nothing different this time, except Charles was somewhat concerned that Abigail seemed different.

Sitting in the waiting room, serious thoughts came to him. *What if something has gone wrong in her back? What if she might need surgery? What if she's sick?*

The nurse wheeled Abigail into the office where the doctor was already seated behind his desk. Charles was also seated, waiting for the report.

"Well, everything appears normal, Abigail," the doctor said. "The results of the blood profile you had taken before coming in shows everything in normal ranges." He glanced over at Charles, giving him a slight smile. "The problem of your tiredness is not anything to be concerned with. It's normal because you are pregnant."

"What!" she exclaimed.

Those words hit Charles like a lightning bolt coming out of a clear blue sky. He didn't know what to say or how to react, except that he suddenly felt chills of happy excitement running all over his body.

"Yes, there's no doubt about it; you are pregnant. You appear to be about three months along," the doctor continued.

"Oh, my goodness," she said rather excitingly, looking at Charles. And just as their eyes met, they broke into big smiles.

"Will there be any problems?" Charles asked. He was concerned that someone in her condition could have a baby in the first place. He never dreamed she could get pregnant.

"I don't think there will be any problems," the doctor responded. "Abigail is young and healthy, and there should be no problems because she is paraplegic. Women with a spinal cord injury can give birth normally, just like any other woman. I want you to make an appointment with your gynecologist. She will take it from here."

He asked if they had any further questions.

They were too stunned and excited to think about asking questions, so he stood up, walked around his desk, and shook hands with them.

"Congratulations," he said, smiling. "You will make fine parents, I'm sure."

Wow, this was another event added to that *something different* that Abigail felt months ago. They were going to have a baby.

The timing for a baby was perfect. Their new career as a team was well-established. The baby would work in well. They had plenty of help in that area. This child was a gift of their faith, and the event fully witnessed that "all things work together for good to [those] who love [God]." Regardless of the threats that came upon them, which could have destroyed their careers, their faith and the reality of God's presence kept them from falling. This new, precious life would overshadow all the suffering.

******

Just as the doctor said, Abigail had a normal delivery without complications. The baby came quickly, as predicted. Hoorays and cheers filled the delivery room as their little baby made its entrance into the world.

Roberto Charles Ricci weighed in at eight pounds, twelve ounces. Charles brought Abigail and Roberto home from the hospital two days later.

Sitting at the piano in the music room, Abigail and the baby comfortably there with him, Charles could find no other song to play than the song he played in praise to God when his crippled right hand was healed—"Great Is Thy Faithfulness."

With deep feeling, he gave the notes the expression he held in his soul—joy and thankfulness. The words in the song could not be more appropriate.

"Great is Thy faithfulness! / Morning by morning new mercies I see; / All I have needed Thy hand hath provided. / Great is Thy faithfulness, Lord, unto me!"[5]

---

5   Thomas O. Chisholm, "Great is Thy Faithfulness," *The Hymnal for Worship & Celebration* (Carol Stream: Hope Publishing Company, 1986).

From The Author

God loves you and has a plan for your life. The Bible says that God loved the world so much that He sent His only Son to die on the cross, so that no one would have to die but all could have eternal life with Him.

We have all sinned and need forgiveness. Jesus died for our sins. He took our place on the cross, so that we could have a right standing with God. If you have never put your faith in Jesus Christ and want to be saved by God's grace in Jesus, His Son, I invite you to pray this prayer and accept Jesus as your Savior:

"Dear God, I realize that I am a sinner. I ask for Your forgiveness. I believe that Jesus is truly Your Son, Who died in my place that I can be saved. I want to put my full trust in Him as my Lord and Savior. I want to follow Him. Take charge of my life now and help me to do Your will. I pray this in the name of Jesus Christ. Amen."

If you have prayed this prayer, God wants you to grow in His grace. Begin by reading the Bible. I suggest starting in the Gospel of John in the New Testament.

God bless you as you daily seek to do God's will and seek His plan for your life.

For more information about
Mary Cates
and
The Same Rainbow's End
please visit:

www.marycatesauthor.com

Ambassador International's mission is to magnify the Lord Jesus Christ and promote His Gospel through the written word.

We believe through the publication of Christian literature, Jesus Christ and His Word will be exalted, believers will be strengthened in their walk with Him, and the lost will be directed to Jesus Christ as the only way of salvation.

For more information about
AMBASSADOR INTERNATIONAL
please visit:

www.ambassador-international.com
@AmbassadorIntl
www.facebook.com/AmbassadorIntl

Thank you for reading this book. Please consider leaving us a review on your favorite retailer's website, Goodreads or Bookbub, or our website.

Cece Burbin thought she knew what love was—people using you to get what they wanted. Until she met Jason Porter. But on what should have been the happiest day of their lives, Cece wakes up in the woods with a lot of pain. Jason is just as frantic to find his lost bride but struggles to trust in God to take care of her. Not realizing he doesn't have much time, Jason sets out to get some answers and to search for love's lost star.

King Solomon is well-known as a wise man and the wealthiest king to have ever lived. But with great power often comes great corruption, and Solomon was no exception—including his collection of wives and concubines. But who were these women? What was life like for them in Solomon's harem? S.A. Jewell dives into a deeper part of Solomon's kingdom and shows how God is always faithful, even when we may doubt His plan.

After Catherine Reed's husband dies, she moves back home in order to accept a new position as the teacher for the town's one-room schoolhouse. Samuel Harris has suffered his own loss and guilt has burdened him ever since. When his old flame comes back to town, he wonders if they can find healing together . . .